THEN CAME YOU

LAWS OF ATTRACTION

KATE MEADER

Then Came You is a work of fiction. Names, places, and incidents either are products of the author's imagination or are used fictitiously. Any resemblance to actual events, locales, or persons, living or dead, is entirely coincidental.

ISBN 9781954107236

To Laurie Oh
For your unfailing support

CHAPTER 1

Aubrey

I hate weddings.

I especially hate friends' weddings. However, I have a peculiar fondness for the groom of this one, Max Henderson, and his girl. Charlie is exactly what he needs—sharp, stylish, and willing to go toe-to-toe with his entitled self. But the last thing *I* need right now is a happy fest when I'd much rather curl up with my kitty, sip on a nice Glenfiddich, and binge watch *Midsomer Murders*. (I have a crush on Tom Barnaby, which probably means my daddy issues are showing atrociously.)

It would look odd if I didn't put in an appearance. Max and I have just figured out how to be friendly again—his fiancée helped—and I really do want to be supportive. Slipping into the church, I reason that I can stay for the ceremony, kiss both parties hello, and skedaddle before the ink is dry on the marriage register.

The pews are full to bursting, but I can make out an empty spot fourth row from the top, exactly where I suspect

Max's friends are situated. I inhale deeply. *Here goes.* Moving closer, I spot the back of Trinity's head and slide into the seat beside her.

"Hey, princess," Lucas, Trinity's boyfriend and one of Max's law firm partners, says with a cheeky grin, while I try to avoid looking beyond him along the pew. If I can't see the problem, it doesn't exist. Tunnel vision will get me through.

Frowning, Trinity touches my upper arm, right above the neon pink cast on my forearm sitting in a matching sling. "Are you okay? What happened?"

"Just me being a dumbass." I squint at the line of hats in front of me, marveling at how Chicagoans at a wedding in November think they're at Royal Ascot. I cast a glance over my shoulder. "Maybe I should sit back there."

No sooner are the words out of my mouth than the air shifts.

"What happened?" a dark voice grits out.

Looking up, I find Grant Lincoln—Max's other partner—staring at me from his place at Lucas's right, the spot I've been avoiding since I parked my ass in this pew. Though it's more like he's sitting on Lucas's lap in an effort to impose himself. His brown hair, tinged with red, is tousled far too early in the day's proceedings. Perhaps he was nervous at the thought of running into me, but that notion doesn't bear up in the face of midnight blue eyes plundering my aplomb, pirate-style.

How unfair that the sight of him should steal my breath every time.

"None of your business."

"How did you get here? Because it looks like you can't drive."

"Big city, Grant. Lots of cabs."

A muscle ticks in his jaw. If I wasn't already so annoyed at being interrogated, I would be appreciating the hell out of that dancing muscle. My ex-husband's not traditionally handsome. People might call him thuggish, even, an image he cultivates to his advantage in court. He's a big guy, broad-shouldered and barrel-chested with a husky voice and attitude to match. When Grant held me in his arms, I felt wrapped in him in the best possible way.

That fuzzy-jagged feeling I get whenever I think of being enveloped in the world that's Grant's arms takes a flying leap through the church's stained-glass windows at his next barked query.

"What are you going to do about going home for Thanksgiving, Bean? Unless you're suddenly okay with flying."

My heart skips at the nickname. At least two years have gone by since I heard it pass his lips. On the day he told me he couldn't do this anymore. Do *us*.

"Nothing for you to worry about," I shoot back.

"You don't like flying?" Trinity asks, all concern. She's the nicest person.

"Um, no." Terrified, actually. "But I'll figure it out."

Grant snorts. Oh, he thinks he knows everything.

Lucas waves a hand between us. "Would you two like to sit together?"

"Certainly not!"

"Hell, no!"

I'll break my other arm before I voluntarily sit beside Grant Roosevelt Lincoln.

TRINITY CONVINCES me to stay for the reception. As I don't want Grant thinking he's driven me away, I channel my mother and pin on my high society smile. Of course we're sitting at the same table, separated by Lucas and Trinity, who are unbelievably cute together.

"So, princess, spill," Lucas says after feeding Trinity a sliver of roasted potato. "Tell us how you broke your arm."

"Oh, y'know. Some idiot kept asking me dumb questions and I lashed out and hit his giant, British head. The usual."

Lucas rolls his eyes, clearly enjoying my dig. He's a funny, egotistical Brit himself. "You need to make up a better story than that, Aubs. Say you tripped over your cat while vacuuming naked."

"Why do you assume I have a cat?"

Grant makes a choking sound. If only.

"Something to say, Lincoln?"

"That thing still alive?"

"Yes, Cat Damon is alive and well, surviving on spite."

"Cat Damon?" Trinity asks. "That's adorable."

"It's a joke." I catch Grant's gaze, piercingly blue and unerringly focused on me. "Or someone's idea of one."

Despite naming my cat, Grant barely tolerated the ball of grump and my kitty hated him right back. Neither of them liked being in competition for my affection. Don't let Mr. Lincoln's southern gentleman demeanor fool you. The lumbering giant with the syrupy voice is the most cutthroat competitor I know, especially in the bedroom.

Three for one was his rule. Three of my orgasms for every one of his. And if he thought I couldn't go the distance, he'd forgo his own. One night I tried faking number three because I was worried he might have a hernia if he didn't get off. He only punished me with two more.

I miss those Grant-given orgasms.

More than that, I miss—no, we won't be taking that trip down memory lane.

THE NIGHT GOES ON. Heartfelt speeches. The first dance. Wedding cake in the kisser. It's all lovely, really, and in time, my curmudgeon self melts away in the face of all the hope and love on display. I can't leave without wishing them well, so I sidle up to Charlie while Max is getting an earful from a woman who looks like his grandmother.

"Nice catch, friend," I whisper in her ear.

"Aubrey!" She turns and hugs me, clearly tipsy on life, love, and Dom Pérignon. "I've been trying to cut my way through the hordes to get to you and your broken limb. What happened?"

"You wouldn't believe me if I told you," I say mysteriously.

She eyes me, and I pray that the alcohol won't compel her to give advice I neither want or need. Perhaps she senses my desire to keep it at a surface level, for her next words are neutral. "Those two next, I think." She nods at the dance floor, where Lucas and Trinity are swaying to Tony Bennett.

"Probably. They had a rough time of it and miraculously made it out the other side."

"The deepest love affairs take work." She pauses. "You know, I'm here—"

"I know!" I plaster on a clown smile. Everyone assumes I'm miserable since my divorce, which was over a year ago. And we were on the rocks for a year before that. I've had plenty of time to get over Grant.

It's the failure that swirls around me like a fog that I can't abide.

"Okay, Aubs, let's dance." Max skirts Charlie and grabs my free hand.

"But, your wife!"

Max stops, his handsome brow furrowed, and leans over to kiss Charlie. "My wife. Can you believe I totally love that? But I can dance with the old ball and chain any day of the week."

Charlie grins. "And so it begins."

I let Max manhandle me onto the dance floor. "You did good, Maxie. Proud of ya."

"Never thought I'd get here. I mean, this is me we're talking about. Anti-marriage, doom and gloom, matrimony is for idiots, and weddings are organized by hucksters." Charlie's a wedding planner by trade so this unholy union with Max the divorce lawyer didn't quite gel from the start. But they soon realized they had more in common than not. His sigh is wistful, and my heart expands with joy, knowing that he's found the woman who'll make him happy.

At least until something rips them apart. Yet I have to think there's hope in this dim, dark world. Perhaps they'll stay on the right side of the one in two that fail.

"You okay?" he asks, his blue eyes softening. "I know you haven't spent much time in the same room as Grant."

"I'm fine. We work in the same building, booze in the same circles, and once, we were really good friends. Maybe we can get back to that."

"You'd have to talk to him first."

"Baby steps. And I talk to him plenty." Out of the side of my mouth across the battlefield in court. And at home when I replay conversations, wishing I'd said *this* and *that* and not *that* and *this*.

"So. Driving home for Thanksgiving?"

I pull back and give him my best Bostonian glare, learned at my grandmother's knee. "Did Grant tell you to ask me that?"

"Nope. I know you hate flying, and you usually drive, so I'm wondering how you're going to do it with your mystery injury."

"Well, there are these big steel machines called . . . trains!"

"They don't allow cats for journeys longer than seven hours."

I stop mid-sway. "How do you know that?"

"Like you, Aubs, my great-aunt Dorothy also likes to take her cat places—"

"You're making this up."

"Great-aunt Dorothy," he insists, the big fat liar, "also likes to take her cat places but was recently stymied on the New York–Miami route. They don't permit the furry beasts in the sleeper cars."

I narrow my eyes. "How fascinating that this one piece of extremely relevant information is right at your fingertips."

"Pub quiz champion. No trivia is beneath my interest. Also . . ." He waves over my shoulder.

I turn to see a large, elderly woman with a white Siamese in her lap. She's stroking it Blofeld-style. "Great-aunt Dorothy?"

"One and the same."

The problem is, I missed Thanksgiving last year. I couldn't stand the thought of rolling up in my car, bearing my sickly cat and the stink of failure. My brothers and their perfect other halves would be held up as the standard-bearers of the Boston Gates, while sad, miserable Aubrey never quite cuts it. It's not as if the demise of my marriage is a secret—well, one person doesn't know—but I haven't had to look anyone in the eye yet and dare them not to judge me.

The Gates don't fail, I can hear my mother saying in her French-tinged whine, which is rather rich, considering my parents' marriage is currently imploding during the longest dissolution ever. And me, a divorce lawyer, just like my ex. Gotta love the irony.

The song ends, but Max holds on to me while the next one starts up.

"I've missed you, Aubs."

"You're only saying that because it's true."

He smiles and I wonder why we never found each other

remotely attractive. Max is a charmer through and through, but he's never once made my heart flutter. Not like—gah!

Grant Roosevelt Lincoln, leave me be.

"I'm so happy for you, old friend. Truly." My voice breaks a little.

He hugs me hard and whispers into my ear, "If he cheated on you, I will kill him."

"No. Nothing like that." Nothing so simple. In truth, for all my grumbling, Grant is the nicest guy on the planet, far too kind for someone like me.

Max's mouth twitches with the need to know. "I never stopped being your friend. I know it was hard with me and Grant working together, but I never stopped."

Max tried to draw me out and back into his life, but I couldn't bear to share my pain with anyone. It's taken me a long time to be fit for company. I'm finally ready to restart life post-GRL.

"Thanks, Maxie. I promise we'll do dinner sometime."

And with a squeeze of his hand, I take my leave.

CHAPTER 2

Grant

She's on the phone near the entrance of The Drake hotel lobby, jet black hair in a fall down her back, wearing a blood-red cocktail dress that maximizes every curve on her petite frame. Curves I know intimately despite the winter coat slung like a cape over her shoulders.

The need to know how she hurt her arm is a barb in my chest, just one more lure that draws me into her orbit. Little Red Riding Hood in the flesh. I suppose that makes me the wolf, but we all know what happened there, don't we?

Didn't end well for the beast.

Spending a single moment in my presence causes her pain, which is why I've made a concerted effort to not be in places where she'll be, other than what's necessary for work. Or at least, I did that for the year after we signed the divorce papers.

My chest squeezes with the effort of avoiding her. But we've made it a year without each other. More than that, because we had to be officially separated before we could dissolve our union. That word, "dissolve"—like we could mix the pain with water, and hey, presto! no more us.

Bullshit, all of it.

In the past couple of months, we've found ourselves at some of the same events, and twice on opposing sides of a case. Even working together in the same building since her law firm moved into the suite five floors above mine. It's eased some of the heartache for me and I want her to get there, too.

After a moment, she ends her call and stares at the phone. I know that move: she just spoke with Marie-Claire, her mother, and knowing this and their history tears at something inside my chest. My need to breathe her air outweighs my desire not to cause her further pain. I've always been a selfish prick where Aubrey is concerned.

"Leaving so soon?"

Her shoulders stiffen and when she turns I know what I'll see: that Bostonian cool she wears so well. On her pivot, I inhale like my lungs could hold on to her scent and use it to fuel me for a few more days. Every time is like the first.

"Thought I should escape before the Hokey Pokey makes an appearance."

"But you always had such great moves."

Unsmiling, she studies me. She knows I have the means to hurt, but she's likely wondering if I have a motive. I'd never do it intentionally but sometimes merely breathing in a person's direction is as harsh as a blow.

Visibly relaxing, she says, "Better than you, for sure. You're an embarrassment on the dance floor."

I chuckle my agreement. "I need room to showcase my talent."

"Yeah, your talent." She smiles tentatively as if she's trying it out after a long time going without, and my heart explodes on the spot. It's been an age since she's graced me with that sun.

I stare, soaking her in while I still can. "Need a ride home?"

"I'll just take a cab." She steps back, toward the revolving door.

Outside, I raise my hand to the guy pulling double duty calling cabs and valets, handing my ticket to him before Aubrey can get a word in. His glance flicks over us and he makes a decision, holding open the passenger door to my car.

Aubrey murmurs, "He thinks we're together."

"Guess we still have that look."

Soap opera super couple. That's what Max called us back in law school. This golden pair who had the world at our feet and a future so bright we had to wear shades.

I tip the valet. "It's just a ride, Aubrey."

She blinks at me and I witness every thought that goes into the decision, the chasm she has to leap across to put it all aside, the rickety bridge she has to build to start that tentative journey. Wordlessly, she settles into the passenger seat.

It's only ten minutes from The Drake to her place in Lincoln Park. I mull over how best to use it. As we merge onto Lake Shore Drive, she's the one to speak first.

"Do you think they'll make it?"

"One in two chance, right?"

"More than that for Max. He'll work at it."

Barely veiled criticism, come on down! I once thought the same until the day I realized that failure might be the only way to keep me sane. She's right about Max, though. Despite the silver spoon upbringing, he's overcome a few obstacles through sheer force of will.

"So, what happened to that girl? The one you brought to Max's cookout?"

She wasn't you. "Didn't work out."

"I'm tough to beat."

"That you are."

She chuckles, low and soft, perhaps pleased at how lighthearted the conversation is. Hell, we're talking about dating other people! Progress, for sure. As long as we're keeping it at surface level then we can pretend the past can't hurt us.

Her amazing legs are bare despite the cool mid-November temps, acres of touchable skin revealed by the upward slide of her dress. My cock stiffens, imagining my hand running up that thigh, in between her legs, spreading her wide as I clamp my palm over that spot where she used to be so needy.

"How's Marie-Claire?" I ask because talking about her mother is about the only thing that can change the direction of my filthy thoughts.

"Was it so obvious?"

I exit onto Fullerton. "Your shoulders get this certain set to them."

"She's her usual high-strung, drive-me-nuts self. Miserable with the effort of divorcing my father and enjoying the drama, too. She's in party planning mode for Libby and making everyone around her insane."

Aubrey's grandmother, Libby, is turning ninety on the Saturday of Thanksgiving weekend, in two weeks.

"Always liked the old bird. She doing okay?"

"She had a fall earlier this year. Broke her hip. It's really slowed her down."

"Hard to imagine anything slowing her down."

"She still doesn't know. About us."

My hands grip the wheel.

"It's just up here on the right," she says, as if I need direction to where my ex-wife lives. I pull into the alleyway beside her building, an Art Deco–inspired structure that suits Aubrey's old-world glamour.

"Aubrey."

Two spots of color tag her cheeks. "She was going through some health issues and no one wanted to upset her. My parents' divorce is stressful enough on everyone and you know how they like to hog the spotlight. I'd planned to tell her about the split in person when I went home last Thanksgiving but I didn't make the trip because my cat had to have kidney surgery. Now I have to fill her in, so I'm planning to tell her when I get there."

This explanation is spilled in a gush.

"I'm surprised your mother hasn't broken the news considering all the joy she feels that we're not together anymore." Marie-Claire has always thought I was about two levels below dog shit and not nearly good enough for the daughter of Bostonian aristocracy.

"I insisted that I be the one to break the news. But every time I got on the phone, Libby would ask about you and talk about how much she adored you." She rolls her eyes at my smirk. "It was just too hard to do it. And now I have to take a train but—"

"You can't take the cat on such a long journey."

"Does everyone know about these Amtrak cat-carrying rules except me?"

It's not like Aubrey to be so disorganized. "So you have to drive." I gesture to her sling. "How did that happen again?"

Ignoring my question, she says, "I suppose you're headed home for the holiday."

"That's the plan."

We used to switch off every year, alternating between ice and fire—and I don't just mean the different climates. Holidays with the Lincolns come with no judgment. With them, Aubrey could finally relax.

"Just kennel the cat and take the train."

"Sure," she says, not because she agrees with me but because she doesn't want to talk about it anymore. That's how Aubrey decides when a discussion has reached its end.

"Thanks for the ride."

She exits the car, leaving the scent of her perfume, a man with a hard-on, and the inklings of a plan.

CHAPTER 3

Grant

"Having sex with the aid of power tools shouldn't be relevant here, Your Honor."

I have to give it to Judge Jamieson: she displays not a jot of surprise at my case's latest turn of events. Instead she redirects from opposing counsel, who just uttered that slightly outrageous statement, and bores a no-quarter-given gaze into me.

"Mr. Lincoln, I'm inclined to agree with counsel for the petitioner. I fail to see how the fact that her client indulged in sexual practices of this nature is relevant."

I prepare to demonstrate exactly how relevant it is. "Your Honor, my client's wife has presented herself as Polyanna—"

"Objection, improper characterization," opposing counsel cuts in.

"As if butter wouldn't melt—" Before she can object again, I rephrase with, "As a woman with vanilla tastes who would be the last person to create a video of herself being penetrated by a sex toy attached to a chainsaw." I turn to opposing counsel and speak to her directly. "Yet she has chosen to paint *my* client as a deviant because he engaged in affairs with multiple partners, to which we've already stipulated. Mrs. Dalton, or should I use her professional name, Shannon Hardwood, is not who she says she is."

The beautiful gray eyes of opposing counsel almost roll out of her head.

"So, she has a hobby. Do you have a problem with what my client does in her spare time? Or perhaps you think the fact she's a woman means her own sexual preferences should be judged more harshly than those of a man?"

"Oh, I have no problem with what your client does in her spare time."

Aubrey addresses the bench. "Then I'd ask the court to rule against admitting this video file into evidence, as it's only evidence of a woman engaging in . . ."

The entire court appears to lean in.

"The achievement of sexual satisfaction, a right of women everywhere."

I snort. Judge Jamieson shoots me her usual hard-ass glare.

"Apologies, Your Honor. Whether or not there's a constitutional right to sexual satisfaction is not settled law."

The judge clears her throat and dryly replies, "Indeed. While Ms. Gates's lofty assertion of female rights in this area is all well and good, that's not the purview of this court. What *is* in my remit is the relevance of this video and Mrs. Dalton's proclivities to this divorce proceeding. If you're just pitting one client's sexual behavior or misbehavior against another's, that won't fly."

Opposing counsel's smirk morphs into a self-satisfied smile.

"Anything else regarding the video, Mr. Lincoln?" the judge asks.

"Actually, yes, Your Honor. As I said, I have no problem with Mrs. Dalton, aka Shannon Hardwood, engaging in activities that bring her immense satisfaction." I turn my head slightly toward Aubrey. "But I do have a problem when a respondent makes money on the achievement of said sexual satisfaction and chooses *not* to include that in her financial statements."

Those eyes flash silver. *Gotcha, Bean.*

While I'd love to spend the day staring at her, maybe even thinking of all the ways I could make her eyes turn to molten mercury, make that curvy body thrum, make that voice whimper and scream in pleasure, now is not the time.

I return my attention to the judge, who clearly doesn't appreciate my exclusion of her from the process. When we're going at it hammer and tongs in a courtroom, it's not unusual for Aubrey and me to forget the world around us.

"Your Honor, Mrs. Dalton, aka Shannon Hardwood, did not declare her income from her 'hobby' to the IRS."

"You have evidence of this income?"

"I do, Your Honor. Along with my client's most recent tax return with a status of married filing jointly." I pass copies of the report from my forensic accountant to the clerk. One goes to Aubrey, another to the judge. "As you can see, Mrs. Dalton, aka Shannon Hard—"

"We know her name, Mr. Lincoln," Aubrey cuts in, clearly pissed as she scans the report.

"Ms. Hardwood has earned close to eighty thousand dollars from her adult streaming channel in the last year. Income she chose not to declare to the IRS or on financial disclosures required during the discovery process."

"Lying bitch whore!" That's my client.

"Pencil dick bastard!" And that would be Aubrey's.

The judge lifts her gaze briefly from the report. "Control your clients, counsel."

"Yes, Your Honor," we both mumble as we respectively soothe the former lovebirds.

While we wait for the judge to finish reading I slide a glance to Aubrey. She's gripping the side of the desk, white-knuckling it so hard her bones might pop through her skin. Aubrey works for Kendall, one of the bigger firms in Chicago, and they have a bevy of forensic accountants and researchers at their disposal. Somehow, she didn't find this out about her client, though I'll admit Mrs. Dalton aka Shannon Hardwood did a fairly decent job of hiding it in an offshore account. Just not good enough to get past my guy.

"Counsel, approach."

I strut to the bar, the clack of Aubrey's heels finding a rhythm with my pulse. She needs those heels so she doesn't look like a munchkin gazing up at the judge. I'm almost tempted to give her a leg up, but if I offered she'd probably stomp one of those stilettos through my foot.

"This doesn't look good for your client's alimony claim, Ms. Gates," Judge Jamieson muses. "It also has implications for the division of assets."

"Your Honor, we'd like time to examine the report and run an investigation of our own."

"Is your client denying she had undeclared income from her business?"

"No, Your Honor, but we'd like to assess . . ."

I remain silent as the judge and Aubrey hash out whether this kills the case or is merely a bump in the road. Mostly, I do this because I love to listen to Bean making an argument. Even now, with her back against the wall, her client exposed, and her case in tatters, her skills are a marvel to behold. I almost feel bad that she's in this position, but not enough to cut her some slack.

Her scent fills my lungs and unfailingly makes my cock twitch and my heart rate quicken. She looks her usual put-together self—that sleek fall of dark hair, the perfect red pout to her lips, the navy pinstriped suit she wears as armor—but there's no missing the half-moons under her eyes. She hasn't been sleeping well. Insomnia was always a problem for her; my fingers, mouth, and cock were invariably the cure.

But I can't help her now.

We don't sleep in the same bed anymore. We don't live in the same house. Somehow our once-perfect lives fell apart and the only time I see her is when she represents the ex of one of my clients or at the odd social run-in like Max's wedding this past weekend.

I live for these days.

Don't get me wrong. It hurts to be around my ex-wife. It hurts knowing she exists in my world but on the periphery. Yet not seeing her at all cuts deeper.

I look up, realizing that the judge is talking to me. "Mr. Lincoln?"

"Yes, Your Honor?"

"Settle this outside of my court?"

My heart hardens and duty to my client kicks in. "My client would prefer we finish this now. Mrs. Dalton aka Shannon Hardwood has clearly endeavored to deceive my client and this court by not revealing a substantial source of income. The claim of alimony should be denied."

"I'm inclined to agree, Mr. Lincoln, but your stunt in dropping this video on the court today without providing it to opposing counsel first is a smidge too flashy for my liking. I love a little excitement as much as the next girl, but not at the expense of process. I'll adjourn to give you both a chance to work this out to everyone's satisfaction." She shoos us both away.

"Lucky," I murmur, so only Aubrey can hear.

"Prick," she sweet-talks right back.

I smile through gritted teeth. "She's not getting a cent,

Aubrey, but we'll throw in a little somethin' to sugar the deal."

She stops at the table I've just turned on her, hand on hip, silver eyes wild. Her breasts heave, a sign she's furious—or turned on. In the past, when we sparred from opposite sides, the sex we had afterward was the best of our lives. Sometimes, we didn't even make it out of the courthouse. Those sinks in the ladies' restroom are the perfect height, and her panties provided just the right amount of friction against my cock as I slid inside her. My favorite place to be.

"What'll you give?" she asks, a little breathlessly.

I lean in and brush my lips against her ear. She shivers, and I imagine she has to clamp her lips closed to rein in a moan.

I know, wishful thinking. Aubrey doesn't think of me that way. Not anymore.

"She can keep the power tools."

CHAPTER 4

Aubrey

She can keep the power tools. Hilarious!

With anyone else, I'd have a little chuckle and wag my finger, but not when Grant is the source. I can't believe we flubbed that background check—we, meaning Kendall, the *supposedly* top-notch firm I work for. Heads are going to roll.

Kendall occupies two floors of a Chicago downtown skyscraper, employs close to a hundred lawyers, and has a stellar reputation. Grant's outfit, where he partners with Max and Lucas, is in the same building, five floors below. They're small, personal, and deal only with family law, primarily divorce. Kendall is more like *LA Law,* dabbling in everything, and I'm the Arnie Becker of the outfit, leading the family law group. Youngest managing associate, too.

Not that my mother cares.

At thirty years old, I should be past this desperate need for my mother's approval. While she vaguely approves that I'm a lawyer, she hates my choice of specialization. There's something unseemly about family law—divorce, in particular. It requires people to air their dirty laundry and that's a big no-no as far as the Gates are concerned. Better I should be dealing with corporate entities. (I could tell my mother that the Supreme Court has decided corporations are people, too, but she would think I was being a smart-ass.)

Stepping into the courthouse elevator, I try not to think of the phone conversation—though "conversation" is a misnomer, given it's one-sidedness—I had with my mother after Max's wedding, but it's hard to ignore the cultured voice that's always played the devil on my shoulder.

"Mason will be at the party, Aubrey. He just bought a house on the Cape."

"And you're telling me this because . . ."

"He's single again." My mother lowered her voice. "And looking."

He could look down his pants and admire his tiny dick for all I care.

"I'm not really on the prowl for Victim No. 2 yet."

She tutted. "It would help to smooth over the inevitable questions about the . . . mistake you made getting married to someone . . . like Grant, cherie."

I suppressed a growl over her dig at my ex. "I didn't say you had to keep my divorce a dirty secret. Just don't tell Libby, who never leaves the tower anyway, until I can tell her myself." My grandmother was practically a recluse. "And no matchmaking. I'm home for Gran."

I still find it hard to believe my mother has somehow kept the sordid secret of my divorce from her Bostonian pearls-clutching social circle. I'm about to bring great shame on the family—or greater than I have up until now. I've always been the dirty secret of the Gates, blessed to have the name but not exactly deserving of it.

Instead of thinking too hard on this, I let my mind

wander to Grant. For the first time in ages, he featured in my fantasies over the weekend.

This shouldn't be a total surprise, but I haven't felt like a sexual being in a long time. Too many bad memories and the only person I wanted to think of that way was the one who I shouldn't. Couldn't. But watching those strong hands of his grip the steering wheel, hearing that buttery drawl slip like silk sheets over my body, just being near him—it opened something in me that I'd been keeping under lock and key.

So, to avoid thoughts of my mother, I think about fucking my ex.

"Ms. Gates."

Damn, the man himself has to appear and ruin a perfectly fine fantasy. He looks like the Terminator in Tom Ford. I can assure you that he didn't dress so well before I met him. He didn't even use chopsticks.

"Mr. Lincoln."

"Oh, hold up, please!" Just before the elevator doors close, Serena Gleason, one of my colleagues at Kendall, joins us inside. She flashes a grin. "Aubrey, heard you got your ass handed to you by—Grant! Didn't see you there." Unlikely, given that the man is about as impossible to miss as a redwood.

"Serena, how you doin'?" Grant's syrup drenches the entire car and he leans in to buss her cheek. "A little birdie told me some lucky guy's scooped you right up. Congratulations."

Serena flashes her hand, showing off a rock the size of a planet. She's marrying her hunky personal trainer. "Thanks, he *is* lucky." Sighing for a couple of seconds at the sight of her ring, she raises her gaze and frowns at me. "What happened to your arm?"

"Nothing."

"Doesn't look like nothing."

"She won't say," Grant offers. "I'm thinking maybe a tryout for the Hawks."

My eye roll is epic.

"Oh, there's a story here." Serena narrows her eyes in suspicion. I'll be a source of gossip, visits from senior partners, and hopefully a tray of cupcakes by five.

The elevator reaches the lobby—finally—and we all step out and stand around awkwardly like we need to discuss our next moves. *Sushi or Italian, friends?*

Serena divides a look between the two of us. "Should I play referee? Or maybe something else?"

I shut that nonsense down immediately. "I'll walk back to the office with you, Rena."

"Got a minute, Bean?"

Again, with that Bean business. I can't. Not now.

Serena mouths "Bean" at me. I want to thump her and stuff that rock on her finger in an uncomfortable place.

Instead, I say sweetly, "No—I need to get back. I've got a client's financials to investigate, remember?"

"Been thinkin' on your dilemma," Grant says, his voice ridiculously lazy and sexy.

"My dilemma?"

"Thanksgiving, traveling with the beast, heading into the Lion's Den."

I shoot a look of *not here* at him, but Serena has already sniffed blood. "The Lion's Den? Color me intrigued!"

He looks amused. "Think you'd prefer we discuss this in private."

"Discuss what? How you tried to bypass discovery in Judge Jamieson's court like a first year associate?"

"Nah. Me driving you to Boston for Thanksgiving so you can pretend to your grandmother that we're still married."

I gasp, which sets off a chain of unfortunate events. Slightly panicked, I move closer to Grant instead of farther away, inhale how good he smells, become light-headed with the pleasure of it, then step back. I look like a dancing fool and Serena definitely notices, her eyes going wide with wonder at my smoothness.

"Rena, I'll catch you later."

"Yeah, you will, girl." Serena toddles off to get the rumor mill grinding at the office.

I shoot stabby eyes at Grant. "Nice going, idiot."

"No problem. Let's get coffee in the food court. Won't take long to sort out the details."

What details? This isn't happening. Yet I turn, trancelike, toward the escalator.

I know he's watching my ass with those dark blue eyes of his. I'm not much taller than five four and I need heels to strike fear and envy. But I've always had a very well-proportioned behind that looks good in pencil skirts and Grant has always been an ass-man.

Like the recent reawakening of my long-dormant sexuality, the sway of my hips as I walk ahead of my ex-husband fills me with power. I know it's ridiculous to feel this way because of a male gaze, but I can't help it. It's *his* gaze that fuels me.

Coffee in hand (I paid for my own, thankyoumuch), I take a seat in the food court and wait for Grant to sit across from me. Ever the contrarian, he pulls a chair around and places it to the side, so he can stretch out his long legs when he sits. Almost like he's presenting . . . *oh.* I can make it out, that hard, left-leaning curve of power. Even at rest, it's impressive.

My mouth waters and I look up to catch him catching me out. What is wrong with me?

"Freak kitchen accident?" he asks.

"Excuse me?"

"Your injury."

I smile sweetly to let him know my lips are sealed on that one. "You were saying . . ."

"Right, me taking you back east. Not such a bad idea, is it? You can't drive with that sling, so either you have to fly, which you won't, or take a train, which you can't. Not if you want to bring that ball of spite. I know you won't kennel him because you can't bear the thought of leaving him behind, especially as he's getting old and sick. I also know that you have to eventually tell Libby about the divorce. She'd react better if we told her together. If she thinks we're both in a good place."

Is that where he thinks we've landed? "Are we? In a good place?"

"I think we're closer to it. First year's the hardest. But we've managed to co-exist at various social events and on elevators for a couple of months now."

True, it's getting better. I'm not sure how I feel about that. "But your own holiday plans?"

"I can visit my mom and sister on the weekend after Libby's birthday party. We can tell her the day after so it doesn't ruin anything for her."

My mother would freak if I turned up with my ex-husband, though it would definitely get her off my back about this matchmaking business.

But . . . it's Grant!

I can barely breathe. "You'd do this? Why?"

He straightens in the chair and leans both elbows on his knees, his face tilted to look at me. His brow crimps and he answers my question with one of his own. "Do they know . . . everything?"

"Everything?"

"Why we parted?"

My heart keens. Just when I thought I could cope with

breathing the same air as him, I'm thrown back to those days when the sight of him signified nothing but failure.

"No. Just the old irreconcilable differences catch-all. Ever handy."

We stare a while, lost in the memories and the pain.

"And I'd rather they didn't know the details," I continue. "I'd rather keep that my—our business."

He nods, his agreement something I can latch onto. Grant has always been more emotional than me, yet I suspect he's never breathed a word of what happened, not even to Max, who would have said something. The dome of pain is reserved for us, and us alone.

He stands and for a moment I think he's going to take me in his arms. I almost welcome it, then feel my heart sink like a stone when he keeps his distance.

"If we were splitting the driving, I'd say we could do it in two days, but with just me, it'd be better in three."

"I haven't said yes."

"Neither have you said no."

I have no answer for that, probably because the thought excites more than it pains.

"Think about it, Bean." Then he walks away, leaving me to watch his most excellent ass in pinstripes. Hey, turnabout's fair play.

CHAPTER 5

Aubrey

"He shouldn't be this upset over two years later, should he?" I squint at my cat, who is curled up on the sofa, currently not displaying any weird behavior whatsoever. Typical. "Once my ex moved out, he seemed okay for a while. Less stressed. And now he's back to his old habits."

"Eating clothes?"

"Destroying them."

"Peeing in shoes?"

"The priciest ones. Somehow he knows."

The animal behaviorist makes a note in her book, then places it in her lap. "Pica, eating non-food items, is very common in stressed-out pets and children."

I know this. I've read every book there is on the topic, enough to earn an animal psychology degree like the woman before me.

"He's especially partial to bras. Just rips them to shreds."

The doc nods thoughtfully, makes another note. "Interesting that his targets are signifiers of femininity." She doesn't say what's interesting about it, just lets it hang in the air.

Is my cat a misogynist?

"He didn't get along with my ex," I say in my defense, or maybe his. "Would hiss when he was around but now . . ."

"Now he's engaging in compulsive behaviors." She makes it sound like this is much worse than hissing. Which, considering the state of my wardrobe, might be right. She looks up from her notebook. "Was your divorce amicable?"

From the Latin *amicus,* meaning *friend.* "I'm a divorce lawyer and so is my ex. While you might hear that word thrown around indiscriminately in the realm of marriage dissolution, it's rarely applicable. People who say their divorces are friendly are usually self-delusional."

She smiles briefly. "So you and he don't talk?"

"We stopped for a while but lately we've been . . . chattier." None of this seems relevant to my cat's behavioral issues yet it's liberating to talk about it with someone neutral. "Grant—that's my ex—is such a good guy, so different from me." I shake my head, a touch embarrassed by that admission. "It's amazing that it worked for so long."

Three years of law school, a year of long-distance dating, and just over three years married. Grant, reserved yet so big-hearted and patient, mapped all the unexplored routes to my heart. He was willing to put in the work to tear down my walls, but in the end there's only so much a man, even one as generous as Grant, could take.

"Are you dating someone now?"

"No."

"Because that kind of change might be good for Cat Damon." She winces in clear disapproval of the name. "While you say he didn't get along with your ex, he probably misses the sight of the two of you together. That cohesive unit gave him comfort. Now that you're alone, he senses *your* stress level and is acting out."

"I'm not stressed about being alone." This outdated notion that everyone has to be paired off is more irksome than my actual singleton status.

"Perhaps I'm overstating it. But he's picking up on something in you."

"So I should screw someone to cure my cat?"

There's no missing her grimace. At two hundred dollars an hour, I thought we'd gotten to that level of comfort. I guess not.

"I think if you're happy, the cat's happ . . . *ier*."

Okay. Mission Fuck Someone to Save the Cat is a go.

"So, tell me about the Maldives. Bet it was gorgeous!"

Charlie grins. "Didn't see much of it. Spent most of the time in the beach cottage getting busy on my honeymoon." She takes a sip of the happy hour sangria we're downing at Cafe Ba-Ba-Reeba, a tapas place in Lincoln Park. "But I'd much rather hear about this road trip you're taking with your ex."

"It's hardly a road trip." It's the *definition* of road trip. "Think of it more as an efficient movement of a car from Point A to Point B. Believe me, if I could drive myself, I would not be involving Grant."

I'm still perplexed that (a) Grant has offered to do this and (b) I didn't refuse outright. Shouldn't he despise me after all these years? We spar like crazy in court, snipe away whenever we're in social situations, and glare at each other across crowded elevators on a semi-regular basis. But underneath it all, I still sense Grant's pity for poor Aubrey who can't even tell her favorite relative a bit of bad news.

"Still keeping mum on the arm injury?" Trinity muses.

"It's not important," I say quickly to hide my embarrassment at how it occurred. "And neither is it important that Grant's doing this."

Two sets of eyes bug out at that statement. Charlie breaks the incredulous silence. "Not important? He's agreeing to spend three days—"

"Two."

"With his ex-wife in an enclosed space. What are you going to talk about?"

"I'll be working on my laptop. He's basically a chauffeur."

"Probably wants to make another go of it," Trinity offers. "So is there anything there worth salvaging?"

Both of them are champing at the bit, dying to ask the *why,* which means I need to divert their attention.

"I'm ready to start dating again."

"Ooh, that's interesting," Trinity coos. "Interesting timing, too."

"Is it?"

"Well, you're going on this road trip and you're probably thinking that if you say your girly bits are spoken for, you won't be tempted."

"That's—that's ridiculous!" And shockingly on point.

Charlie laughs knowingly.

"Oh, shut it, smug married person! So I've been feeling sort of . . ." They lean in. "Horny," I hiss. "All right. Freakin' horny. It's been a while since I've wanted to do anything other than work or sleep or"—*move from the sofa to the bed and back again every weekend*—"just veg out. And I've started feeling frisky, I suppose, and my cat's psychologist thinks it might be good for him to see me with another man."

Trinity rolls in her lips. "Your what now?"

"My cat psychologist. Officially she's an animal behaviorist. Cat Damon's been acting out a lot more than usual and she thinks it's because he misses . . . well, you know."

"Grant?" Charlie's mouth twists. "The cat shrink is able to tell all this?"

I gush out a long sigh. "She listens and doesn't judge."

Charlie looks like a lightbulb has gone off. "So this is a way of getting sneaky therapy for *you*?"

"Yes! It's cheaper, too."

"And it doesn't require any accountability or progress on your part because technically she's treating the cat," Charlie adds.

Technically. God, this is so messed up: I'm currently in sneak therapy with my cat's psychologist. "And her conclusion—*to help my cat*—means I'm looking for a good, hard man to get me juiced up."

Trinity raises her glass. "To good, hard men, especially ones prescribed by cat psychologists."

I drink to that, gearing up to my next damning admission. "I've been dreaming about him. Grant."

Charlie shrugs. "That's not unusual, is it? You saw him at the wedding."

Trinity gets there quicker. "You mean *sex* dreams?"

"Uh, speak louder. They didn't hear you over on the other side of the restaurant."

The girls are all agog. "That's why you want to start dating again," Charlie says. "Because you're hot for your ex, you horny devil."

I sigh, resigned to their conclusion. "It's just familiarity, really. I know what that body looks like, what that cock feels like, how good the damn orgasms were. Sex was never a problem for Grant and me."

"So what was?" Charlie flicks a quick glance at Trinity. "You were married for what . . . three years? Together longer than that. Did he fuck up?"

Everyone assumes Grant cheated on me, or they make this assumption to avoid asking the tacky question of whether *I* cheated on him. Inevitably the credit for a marriage's breakdown is unfairly gendered. The guy couldn't keep it in his pants, obviously.

"He didn't fuck up. We both reached a point where being together hurt more than being apart."

Simultaneously, they grasp my hand. While they can sympathize, neither of them can truly understand. They're both so madly, deeply in love and nothing can pierce that. Nothing *should* pierce it. I'm happy for them and I want them to succeed.

I'm also ready to move on with my own life. Perhaps I can put some of the demons of my marriage to rest during this road trip. And if knowing my ex-husband is on the other side of the wall of a hotel room helps fuel an orgasm or two, I'll take it as an early holiday gift.

CHAPTER 6

Aubrey

What does a girl pack for a road trip to see her dysfunctional family and crazy grandmother while shotgunning it with a certifiable cat and the ex who should be running in the other direction?

On the bed, I place the following items into evidence:

Thai Lime and Chili Almonds

Milk Chocolate S'mashing S'mores

Crunchy swirls (made with lentils, Your Honor, so they're healthy-*er*.)

Trader Joe's snacks sorted, I consider the clothes I need. Nothing sexy, because what would be the point? As attracted as I still am to Grant—and how unfair is that?—it's a ditch I do not want to travel.

I frown at Cat Damon, who's eyeing a Fendi slingback pump with intent.

"Don't even think about it. I got those at eighty percent off, which makes them more valuable to me than if they'd been full price." A bargain remembered fondly warms the coldest heart.

My kitty opens his mouth to comment. "Arghhh."

He sounds like a pirate, Bean. A cranky, three-packs-a-day, parrot-sporting pirate.

I pull out my carry-on from the closet and another memory assaults me. The last time I used this suitcase—nearly two years ago—it wasn't empty . . .

Like a horror movie queen creeping down to the dark, dank basement, I unzip the carry-on with trembling fingers. *Buck up, Aubrey. It's just a suitcase!*

Nothing. As empty as the void behind my rib cage, ready to be filled, the potential of a trip laid out bare. But the last time, its contents signified a different potential. A life snuffed out, a fate twisted.

Back then, it was closer to the Christmas holidays, and I'd just arrived home laden with shopping bags, filled with gifts I needed to wrap and send to my family for the holidays. I'd have to overnight them because I'd left it so late, and we were headed to Helen, Georgia, in the morning to spend the holiday with Grant's family.

So much to do! Packing and wrapping and a playlist for the car, cheery holiday songs to cover the once companionable, now awkward silences. (Grant liked to pretend he hated Christmas music but there was no stopping him once Mariah warble-wormed her way into his ear.) We just needed another month to leapfrog the jagged rocks, skirt the quicksand, and land on solid ground. There'd be a pothole or two, but we'd navigate those more easily once we got through the holidays.

I caught sight of myself in the hallway mirror, my slim frame in the drop-dead gorgeous Badgley Mischka suit. My hand went to my stomach. Flat as a board, like it had never happened. I'd recovered quickly, my body telling me to get a move on. *To get over it.*

And I would. Shaking my head, half-determination in the gesture, I opened the bedroom closet, pulled out one of the carry-ons, and unzipped it. A couple of shopping bags lay inside, and curious, I opened the first one.

A gasp escaped me.

I picked up one pair of cute little booties with satin ribbons, marveling at their softness. And the colors? A beautiful rainbow of pastels like something out of a children's book. In another bag I found a tutu, its frilly skirt like an Elizabethan neck ruffle. And—oh!—a Cubs onesie, possibly the most adorable thing I'd ever seen.

Each reveal stabbed deep, feeling like the worst gift giving ever. An anti-holiday. These things looked like they would better fit a doll rather than a living, breathing—

"Hey," I heard behind me, the greeting pinning me in place. I couldn't turn. I couldn't meet his accusing gaze.

Gently, Grant took the onesie out of my hands, which had locked up like a crone's claws on the soft fabric. "I just saw this stuff and couldn't help myself. Forgot it was here, to be honest." His voice sounded rusty.

Tentatively, I slanted a look. He looked tired. Haunted.

"Grant—" I had no clue how to respond. A normal woman would have cried at seeing these reminders of a dad-to-be's pride, but shock wouldn't permit me to react. Vaguely, I was aware of him putting the relics of our loss into a bag and then he left the room, to hide them from me, perhaps.

When he returned, I was still in the same place. He sat on the bed. "I'm sorry you had to see that. I should've taken care of it ages ago."

"It's okay," I whispered. "I was starting to pack for the trip and . . ." I waved ineffectually at the suitcase, as if he couldn't put two and two together himself. Needing to occupy my hands, I yanked open my underwear drawer, conscious that it might be hiding some other horror I was unprepared for. "I'm sorry about missing the appointment. The shit hit the fan with one of my clients showing up at the office out of the blue."

"That's the third time we've had to cancel," he said wearily. "If you don't want to do this, you need to tell me."

"I do!" My enthusiasm was a little over the top given the circumstances—or perhaps because of them. Who was dying to engage in couples' therapy to discuss a miscarriage? After what I'd just seen, though, it seemed like Grant needed this more than I did. I wasn't the one hoarding adorable baby clothes in a closet.

"She said that we should reassess if this is what we really want," Grant continued. "That we both have to be on board."

"It's just that the holidays are the worst time to be starting this. We're both so busy with our caseloads and plans for the trip." The words dried up under the weight of Grant's silent censure. "Don't look at me like that."

"Like what?"

"Like I'm a freak for not wanting to spill my guts to a stranger."

I couldn't even cry at the sight of a Cubs onesie. I couldn't cry at all. Every part of me was numb, especially my tear ducts.

"Did you ever have any intention of going to therapy? Or are you expecting me to forget about it?" He could mean the therapy, the miscarriage, or us.

I wanted to scream, *Why can't you forget? Why can't we just move on?*

But I couldn't say that. Marriage, the work of it—and boy was it work, lately—required that we respected each other's grieving process, though it seemed his carried more weight than mine.

He bought clothes for our baby.

Resentment that I had to do this his way bit my neck. "I need to get ready for the trip."

Cat Damon gave a whiny complaint. I swore he picked up on the thick tension between us.

"Don't want to go, do you, kitty?" I stroked his back and picked him up, putting him in the suitcase while I chose which panties would be appropriate for staying with my mother-in-law. They were no longer useful for seducing my husband. Believe me, I'd tried. "You'd rather stay here, wouldn't you?"

"Which one of you does that apply to?" Grant muttered.

"Well, I can't say it's going to be easy. Your mom will know something's wro—not quite right." I'd asked Grant not to share what happened with our families or friends. We'd withdrawn from them in the last couple of months, but the true test would be with Sherry. Grant's connection to her was so strong that I didn't see how we could fool those insightful eyes of hers.

Strange to say it, but it would've been easier to spend the holiday with my crab-hearted family where no one said what they meant or cared to probe deeper.

"She could help, you know? My mom. She's good at that kind of thing. Loves you like her own."

And I adored her. "Sneak some therapy in over the holidays?"

"God knows nothing I'm saying is working."

The words cut me deep, not just that he was hurting but that I was the cause of it. Lately, it all felt like my fault. The ditch was deep and unclimbable, and I couldn't gain purchase on the slippery sides. "We tell our clients time and tears. We're going to get there, Grant."

"You don't want to go home, do you?" He meant his home in Helen, Georgia.

I didn't answer, which was answer enough. I wanted to crawl under the covers and sleep forever.

"Aubrey, I—" He scrubbed a hand through his hair, mussing it in a way that made my hands itch to smooth. To soothe him. "I can't do this anymore. I feel like we're having the same argument over and over."

"If you'd just let it play out, Grant—"

"No, Bean." He stood, his usual solidity somehow diminished. The guilt I felt in that moment crushed me. *I'd done that.* "No."

He was right about the same argument. We'd already had it, once, three times, ten. We might change the verbiage and shift the emphasis onto different words, but the crux of it was the same: He wanted vivisection, I wanted a burial.

Sometime in the middle of the night, he left for Georgia, leaving behind a Post-it note telling me to take some time to think. But that was the problem right there: I didn't want to think at all. I wanted to feel safe in my husband's arms with his body taking charge of my pain, our mutual desire dulling the worst of it.

I wanted to block out however long it took me to be normal again.

But that time to think turned into time to fail. My husband never returned to our home, and a few weeks later I began the process to formally separate. To sever those last threads bonding us. Together in our tomb of a marriage, I was only hurting him.

And now we're back, full circle with another road trip, another holiday. Grant will be here any moment and I'll be ready with my suitcase full of gifts and snacks and potential.

CHAPTER 7

Grant

I'm outside Aubrey's place on the Monday morning before Thanksgiving, letting the engine idle and psyching myself up for the journey ahead.

Am I out of my ever-loving-mind?

Three days in a car with my ex-wife and her demon cat. Three days of her scent and her sighs, her surface-level conversation and bone-deep condescension to keep the hurt at bay. When I told Max, he responded exactly as I suspected he would: *Good luck*. He's never pried about our breakup, just accepted it as inevitable. But since he found Charlie, I see him foaming at the mouth to know.

How can I explain when I hardly know myself?

So there was an inciting event, but plenty of couples get through their pain. If they're strong enough, they overcome the lows. I thought we were strong enough. I was wrong.

Admitting that to my friend would have killed me. It's taken me over a year to admit it to myself.

Lucas, on the other hand, grinned in that inane British

cheeky chappy way of his. No good luck or well wishes from him, just a recommendation to bring condoms. Idiot.

It's weird to see my partners so loved up, the last two guys I'd expect to find lifelong happiness with another person. Of course, there are no guarantees. I'm the poster boy for that.

My phone buzzes and I can't help smiling at the face I see materializing on my screen.

"What's up, Bug?"

"Don't call me that!" My eight-year-old sister, Zoe, rolls her eyes as only eight-year-olds can do. "I'm too old for it."

"But you thought it was cute last month."

"Exactly. Last month," she says with all the wisdom that a month older can give. "Mom said you're not coming home for Thanksgiving!"

I wince. "I am, but remember, the holiday is an entire weekend. I'll make it there on Sunday." I intend to fly down after Libby's party, then back up to drive Aubrey home.

"When it's over!"

Such drama, but that's my little sis. She adores me, which is understandable because I'm awesome, but less understandable considering our age difference of twenty-three years. My momma married Jake during my second year of law school, then along came Zoe—or Bug as I called her from the start. Perfect timing, really, because damn, I'd been worried about my momma all alone back home. It had always been the two of us against the world. The woman made a shitload of sacrifices to get me where I am, so God knows meeting a good guy like Jake was the best thing that could have happened to her. Until Zoe, that is.

"I've got something for you, but if you're going to whine . . ."

That tune changes faster than a tick. "I won't! I won't! What is it?"

"A surprise, and that's all I'm gonna say. Hey, is Momma there?"

"I'm here, hon!" Of course she is. At forty-seven, it's hard to believe she has a thirty-one year old son. She's still young and energetic, shining brightly with her naturally blond hair and sparkling blue eyes. "Now, I don't often agree with your sister, but she's right on this. You should be home with your family for the holiday." She lowers her voice. "Where you're wanted. Do they even serve turkey up there or is it somethin' fancy like filet mignon and lobster for luncheon?"

Sherry usually equates imagined class differences in food terms. She's met Aubrey's parents only once and she was less than impressed.

"Momma, I'm just doing Aubrey a favor. She hurt her arm and can't drive and it's important she get to Boston to see her grandmother. The woman's knocking ninety after all."

"I know, I know! God, you're nothin' but a sucker for that girl." She sees my frown, and quickly amends. "I just don't want you to get hurt." The tacked-on *again* is unspoken.

"We're just friends. This is a couple of buddies helping each other out."

"You ain't never once looked at that girl like she was your buddy, Grant Roosevelt Lincoln."

She's right. I fell hard for her and only in the last couple of months have I had the strength to get up. A woman like Aubrey can level a man.

As if conjured, the heartbreaker herself appears at the front door to her building, cat carrier case in hand. She's wearing my favorite red coat, the one that makes her look like a wicked fairy-tale character, walking in the woods, cruising for trouble. But it's draped over her shoulders because of the sling. She must be freezing.

"Momma, I gotta go. I'll check in on Thanksgiving. Say hi to Jake and bye to Zoe for me."

"All right—" But I'm already hanging up as I jump out of the SUV.

"You should have taken a cab," Aubrey says, frowning over my shoulder. "You'll never get parking around here."

"Don't need to. We're taking my car."

She narrows her eyes. "No . . . no, we should go in mine."

"I don't like your car."

"You've never even driven it."

"Exactly." I approach the cat carrier, now placed at her feet. "Hey, you little ball of bile, how ya doin'?"

"M#%*&!" Ever the charmer, the cat always sounds like he's cussin' me out. He follows up with a hiss in case I have any doubts.

"He knows you hate him," Aubrey says, her tone a touch gleeful. "You're going to have to do better than that."

I hunker down and meet the cat, a tabby with 'tude, on level terms. Around his right eye, the fur is darker, giving him the look of a pirate, complete with patch. He's got to be at least ten years old, and Christ, he's never liked me, even though I rescued the little prick. Do you think he appreciates it? That'd be a hard no.

"Hey, buddy, ready for a road trip?"

The hiss evolves to a growl.

I stand. "Think we understand each other."

"He'll feel better in the back of my car. More familiar."

"I'm driving, so it's mine or nothing."

She sets her mouth in that way that makes me want to kiss it, plunder it, do filthy-gorgeous things to it. "Fine."

Ten minutes later we're already arguing about the music, or rather, Aubrey is. I'm staying out of it.

"I've already said I don't care which station you play."

"But all your channels are set to classic rock and—ugh—country."

"So find another one you like."

She grumbles, muttering things like "typical" and "difficult." I don't challenge her, because I know she's nervous. This is Aubrey's way of settling in.

She opens up her phone. "I've mapped the route. I expect we can make Buffalo by dinnertime."

"We'll be stopping in Cleveland, Bean."

"But that's only a third of the way. If we press on to Buffalo, we could do this in two days."

"You really want to see your mother a day early?"

She looks out the window. "She's not that bad."

My silence substitutes for commentary.

"She just has certain expectations."

"Which no one can ever meet." I'm talking about myself but I may as well be speaking of Aubrey and her entire family. Not ready to fight with her on this—plenty of time for that—I change the subject. "I want to hit the Rock and Roll Hall of Fame, so Cleveland it is. Besides, I told you this would take three days."

"I know, but . . ." She pauses. "Cat Damon won't like it."

Aubrey won't like it, she means. I don't care. My car, my rules.

My Aubrey, my plan.

What's the plan? I'm not sure yet. But I need time to crack her shell, to find the woman I fell in love with the first moment I laid eyes on her. Two days won't be enough.

She adjusts the radio dials again, looking for something that appeals to her. She finally lands on NPR, where they're talking about the science of sleep. The gist of the piece is that you need eight hours a night and don't even think about trying to compensate by sleeping extra on the weekends. Your body won't fall for that scam.

"You sleeping well these days?" I ask.

"Okay."

I slide a glance at her, noting the perfect pink tinge to her cheeks, flushed with the heat in the car. When she had problems sleeping, usually because she worried about everything —her career, her cases, her clients, her bosses, her parents, her brothers, her grandmother, her cat—I'd take charge with the Grant Sleep Solution.

"Not getting enough orgasms, Bean?"

"Knew it wouldn't take long."

"What?"

"Sex, Grant. I knew it wouldn't take long for you to bring up sex. Let's be clear. You and I will not be connecting our genitals on this trip."

"You old romantic, you."

"I'm serious. Just because—" She cuts off.

"Just because what, Bean?"

She makes a sound of annoyance, sort of like the cat. "And that Bean business. You can stop that, too."

"It's your name."

"No, it's not. It's a dumb nickname you came up with because—" She stops, evidently remembering why I came up with it and the night I explained it. Thoroughly. She fumbles in her bag and pulls out her laptop. "I have work to do, so silence would be appreciated."

"Sure thing, Bean."

"Grant!" But she's laughing at my orneriness. "Why are you so damn stubborn?"

"We both are. It's why the sex was so great. Neither one of us ever wanted to give in."

She's firing up her laptop. "Well, stubborn didn't work so great outside the bedroom."

Thing is, we were pretty good in every other room of the house, too. Aubrey liked to have her way and for the most part I let her. As long as she let me lead when it came to her pleasure, the rest was always negotiable. Except now I know what I did wrong. I should have pushed back more, taken a firmer hand in managing her grief.

Our grief.

If we'd shared that grief with anyone beyond our bubble of two, I know what they would have said: it wasn't a real child. Just a mass of cells, hardly formed. But we both knew different.

Aubrey miscarried in her eighth week. But that for brief time we were pregnant, I was happier than I'd ever been. We were buoyant and our fledgling hope was crushed too soon.

I lost a child, and in the process, I lost the love of my life.

CHAPTER 8

Aubrey

The snow starts about a hundred miles outside of Cleveland, great big wet clumps that slow everything down. Cars fishtail ahead of us, and we pass a fair number of fender benders and spinouts. It's only two in the afternoon but the skies are ominous.

I should have taken the train, snuck Cat Damon on somehow, because this is dangerous. But whenever I slide a glance to Grant, I find his usual rock-solid self. Midnight blue eyes on the road, that strong brow set to focus. He used to be clean-shaven, but not anymore. Facial hair has never appealed to me, but on Grant, hell yeah. I always thought smooth was his attempt to fit in with the clean-cut boys in law school, and later those men he'd encounter in the courtroom. The stubble suits him better.

Nothing has ever phased him, and God knows I tried to knock him off his stilts. Resisting Grant has been my greatest challenge, though when we started dating it was him resisting me.

Just two weeks into our first year in law school and Grant had taken me out to dinner three times, playing the perfect southern gent through every date. It was, shall we say, frustrating as heck. I was the first to admit that I could come off as aloof. Was I doing that with Grant? I didn't know. Around him, I felt hot and excited. Shaky and strange.

Getting to know him had been a joy because he was ostensibly reserved, yet effusive about things he cared about. Close to his mom, he worried like hell about her. She had a new boyfriend and Grant wasn't sure he liked him—yet.

"You're protective of your mom," I observed. "That's cute."

He blushed, and damn, *that* was cute.

It was Saturday—date night around the world—and Grant was scheduled to pick me up at my place. He hadn't seen my apartment, wouldn't even come up after taking me out. We had yet to kiss beyond a quick peck to my cheek.

Good thing I had a plan.

I smoothed my dress down my thighs and did a quick turn to check out my legs and heels—red Louboutins that made me look ten feet tall. Still not enough to reach Grant's lips so he was going to have to compromise and come down to my filthy, nympho level.

The intercom buzzed. "Hello?"

"It's Grant."

"Come on up."

My heart jumped into my throat and an eternity ticked by before he pushed back the ajar door. But Grant's face wasn't the first I saw. That honor went to the ugliest creature in existence, a cat—maybe?—with an expression of undeniable grumpiness and a life hard-bitten.

"Who's this?"

"I found him outside."

My heart melted at the sight of this helpless creature

cradled in Grant's big, protective arms. I was also a wee bit jealous because that kitty was seeing more action than me. "We should feed it. She's probably starving."

"It's a he." Grant followed me into the kitchen, and my seduction plans fell by the wayside, or so I thought. When I turned, however, I found him watching my legs.

He raised his gaze to my face. "You are absolutely gorgeous, Bean."

I swallowed, bowled over by the compliment, even though I knew I looked good. Had I not planned it after all? Grant had a way of looking at me that was thorough and all-encompassing, yet he had never touched me. Didn't he want me as much as I wanted him?

"Milk?"

"Say 'gain?"

I nodded at his precious bundle. "For our guest."

"Good start."

I filled a soup bowl with milk and lay it on the floor. Grant placed the cat in front of the bowl. Two sniffs and he was in.

"Do you think he has an owner?"

"Probably not. This is a street cat."

Right now he was a hungry cat. I watched the furry ball, then caught Grant's eye, firmly and unabashedly locked on me.

"What?"

"You make it very hard to be a gentleman around you."

"Who says you have to be a gentleman?"

He leaned against the counter, his hands behind his back. "I do. A woman like you deserves to be treated like a queen."

My heart fluttered madly, though I was torn about the "woman like you" comment. I loved being on this pedestal built by Grant but would happily tumble off it into his strong arms. "Sometimes queens need to be treated a little less royally."

A muscle went bananas in his jaw and a flush of heat flagged his cheekbones. Biceps bulged indecently against the fabric of his striped blue Oxford, as if he was flexing or . . . oh! He was *gripping* the counter behind him.

"Are you trying *not* to touch me?"

"If I touch you," he gritted out, more animal than I'd ever heard from a human, "you'll be out of that dress in ten seconds."

A savage kick of lust almost paralyzed me.

"Not even time for a kiss?" I approached, carefully, as one would a caged beast, and placed my hands on his unyielding chest. His heart beat hard and vibrantly under my fingertips.

"Aubrey, I'm trying—"

"To not jump me?"

"To not ravage you. You're so tiny and I'm so . . . not."

But I loved that. I adored his burly size compared to my slight frame. I wanted him to pick me up and wrap me up and fuck me up. I wanted him to act on that ravaging instinct.

On tiptoes, I kissed him and took what was coming to me. What I'd been waiting on for weeks. Maybe years. He kissed me back with such ferocity my skin sizzled all the way down to my toes. Our tongues twined, setting fire to the kindling we'd been building for weeks. Three more seconds and his hands were on my butt, lifting me onto the kitchen island, which created the perfect height and fit for us to come together at last.

"We're past ten seconds and I'm still wearing this dress, Georgia. Guess I'm not as tempting as you claimed."

He drew back, panting hard, his eyes raking me thoroughly. "It looks expensive."

"It is. I bought it with plans to seduce you. And it looks like it's working."

He sucked my lower lip into his mouth, held it, then traced soothing kisses along the seam. "I find that maybe I have it in me to torture you for a while."

"You've only been doing it since the day we met. I've been dying for you to touch me. Anything!" This desperation was so unlike me. I kind of liked it.

Our guest meowed just then, a plaintive sound that drew our attention.

"Do you think he'll be okay for a while?" I asked Grant.

"What's a while?"

"As long as it takes you to make me come. Twice."

His nostrils flared, and for a moment I worried I was too forward. Maybe he preferred polite southern belles and didn't enjoy uppity women who stated their needs so brashly. If my mother could've heard me, she'd have turned over in the coffin she slept in at night.

Strong fingers dug into my butt and dragged me close. "Twice, huh?" He picked me up, hitched my legs over his firm hips, and started walking, his gaze eating me alive with every step. Somehow, despite this being his first visit, he knew the floor plan of my apartment without the need to look over my shoulder. He placed me gently on the sofa.

I pointed to my right. "Bedroom's through there."

"Not a good idea." Two king-sized hands separated my thighs and pushed up my dress.

"But—"

"If we go into the bedroom it'll be too fast. Too desperate."

Sounded fine to me.

"And I need to savor you."

I liked that word on his lips. *Savor.* I liked his next move as well—the one where he hooked a finger in my black silk thong and inched it down. I especially liked how his hand shook, possibly from the effort not to rip it off.

My hem was up around my hips and there was no place to hide. With palms spreading me wide, he focused on my slick nakedness, so intently and for so long that I started to breathe in shallow spurts.

"Grant, please touch me."

Kneading my thighs, he slid his thumbs toward my center. A lick of his lips told me he liked what he saw, how I felt beneath his hands, the reaction he was producing. My hips swiveled in invitation, a desire to create some friction.

"What do you need, Bean?"

I'd once assumed he called me that because I came from Boston, but he'd assured me that he had another reason. "Wh—what's that mean? Bean?"

He snatched a breath. "Because you're petite, as cute as a bean, all this potential that's not quite fully realized, but you're going to bloom into something wonderful. With the right care and feeding." He slicked a thumb on the outer folds of my pussy, separating as he mapped each liquid-filled well of flesh. The touch was soft, yet methodical, and when he glanced over my clit, I bucked off the sofa. "This little nub of flesh is like a bean that's hiding all your power, Aubrey."

Weird as hell, yet I loved every word.

He stroked my clit again, his gaze on me as he assessed my response. I knew what I liked but I'd never told anyone in detail. Had never even let a guy go down on me.

I was going to let Grant. I was probably going to beg him.

"Pussy power," I whispered, buying into the fantasy he presented as fact.

"That's it, Bean. Claim it. Tell me what you need."

Still he stroked my pulsing clit (I refused to call it bean!) but in a way that was too gentle to get me to that peak.

"Any good with your tongue, Georgia?"

The corner of his mouth kicked up. "Guess you haven't been listening in class."

Oh, but I had. Grant was the smartest, sharpest guy I'd ever met. When he spoke during lectures, I was mesmerized at all that slow treacle dripping over incisive commentary.

"You're going to have to spell it out, Aubrey. Specificity is key when it comes to the law." He slipped a finger inside me, stretching my walls, previewing coming attractions.

"More, I need more."

"More what?"

"Fingers, tongue." *Your cock, your words, your shelter.*

I had brothers who didn't do their job, parents who barely noticed me. Independence was instilled in me from a young age, an innate survivalist streak, but right now I needed to be seen. Grant's calm reacted to forces raging within me, forces I'd spent my life suppressing.

Another finger inside, his head bent to where I needed him most. Both fingers thrust in delicious rhythm, and finally, finally, he licked me. My body ignited at that touch, and the hunger between us exploded. I came in a frankly embarrassing instant.

His heavy-lidded eyes met mine.

"Damn, I love when you let go, Bean. Gonna need more of that."

He placed the heel of his hand over me and spread my liquid desire around, sparking the perfect build to a second orgasm. I wasn't the speed queen this go-around, and somehow that made it better. Or more likely, it was Grant's laser-eyed focus on me the entire time. On the descent, I grabbed his tie to pull him in for a kiss and felt his moan all the way to my heart.

"Let me touch you," I said. "Fuck me properly."

"You've had enough."

"But, you."

I cupped his erection through his pants, all that pulsing power that seemed to swell in my hand. "You need this, too, Grant."

White hot desire ravaged his features and briefly he closed his eyes, my touch clearly too much. Owning him like this, the glory of it, thrilled through me.

"Say it, Grant. Say you need it."

He nodded, then a strangled "yes" emerged with the opening of his dark blue eyes.

Pushing him back, I straddled him, pulling my dress over my head at the same time. My La Perla bra did a decent job of hiking up my small breasts, but I guess inadequacy was in the eye of the possessor—Grant's gaze went wide and wanting.

He glanced a thumb over the hard peak thorough the silk. "You're so perfect."

I knew I wasn't, that every day I strove for some fucked-up version of perfection in answer to my parents' siren call, the one that insisted I wasn't good enough to bear the Gates name. I must have revealed something in my expression because Grant cupped my face and melded my gaze with his.

"It doesn't matter what happens outside of us. There'll always be obstacles but you tell me what you need, what you want, and what you desire, and inside this, *inside us,* I will make it happen. I will make it perfect. Do you understand, Aubrey?"

I didn't, but I wanted to. I craved the assurance that oozed from his pores.

"Right now, I want you inside me." I was used to doing things quickly, efficiently, getting to the point. Dwelling was not the Yankee way.

Tell that to my man from the South.

"I'll go slow, baby. Give you time to take me in."

Sure thing, Mr. Braggart, I thought as I unzipped and

unpacked—whoa, that's some mighty fine equipment you have there! I had no doubt we'd fit, but Grant was already there, teasing with his fingers between my thighs, ensuring I'd be slick enough to take him deep. He handed me the condom, and boy, I had a job of it, but then, then, *then,* it was happening.

Torturously.

Oh, God, please. Inch by beautiful inch, Grant stole his way into my body and into my heart. The feel of him stretching me, challenging me to work with him, was exquisite.

It would be the story of us.

"Jesus, feels so fucking good."

It was the first time I'd heard him swear. He was a different man when stoked this way.

I moved up, and with each downward stroke accepted more of him. So hot, so deep, so perfect. His hands on my ass controlled the rhythm, the sweet friction sent waves of pleasure rolling through me. I sank down deep and held still for one precious, golden moment of connection.

"Is—is this what it'll always be like?" I panted, almost ashamed at my show of vulnerability but desperately needing to know. *Promise me it will always be perfect. That we're a team. That we're forever.*

"I'm thinking three."

"Three what?"

Stilling my sensual rock, he lifted my hand from his shoulder and placed a kiss on my wrist, another on my palm, and a final one on the tip of my index finger. It was unbearably erotic, even more so than the fact he was balls-deep inside me.

"Two girls and a boy, don't mind the order."

I gasped. He smiled.

"You can't just say that."

"Can and did."

And in that moment, I reached that peak and saw it. Our entire lives spread out before us, shining and beautiful. Three bundles of joy with sparkling blue eyes and Grant's shy smile. I wanted it so much that I forgave him the lie. Like me, he was caught up in the power of it.

Because no one, not even a man as sure as Grant Roosevelt Lincoln, can truly promise forever.

CHAPTER 9

Aubrey

Once in Cleveland, we check into our separate rooms. I informed Grant I wanted a night in and I'd see him for breakfast in the morning, but it's not long before I get antsy, needing to be among people, even if it's only at the hotel bar, anonymous in an anonymous city. (Sorry, Cleveland, I'm sure you're lovely beneath all that snow.)

My second dirty martini appears before I've finished my first. I turn to find him at the end of the bar, and my breath catches just as it did that first day I saw him in the lecture hall. How does he do it? More to the point, how *dare* he do it?

He raises his beer bottle—Budweiser, Grant doesn't care for anything crafty—and gives me that slow, shy smile, the one guaranteed to heat me from the inside out and make my panties slip an inch or two. These days, it takes more than that for the full-scale underwear drop. I've become more circumspect in my old age.

I raise my glass back and shift my thigh so my skirt rides up a little. It's deliberate, an invitation. In a few seconds, the seat beside me is host to the most excellent ass I've ever had the pleasure of fondling. To think those gorgeous buns were all mine for the exploring and gripping and biting—

Hold up there, Gates.

There will be no butt-grabbing or ass-nibbling shenanigans with your ex-husband!

But said ex-husband has always had a way with words. "Want to screw ourselves stupid in my hotel room?"

I almost choke on an olive. A resounding clap on the back coughs it up from my throat, whereupon I deposit it on a napkin. First off, I give it an accusing glare as if that spherical blob is to blame for the less than sophisticated response to what I just heard.

"Ever heard of foreplay?"

He raises an eyebrow. "Seven hours in the car with your whining cat. All the foreplay I need."

I laugh my head off. The muscles in my belly constrict, questioning this burst of energy, and I realize it's been a long time since I let loose like this.

"All right, all right, let's try again," he drawls. "Waiting for someone?"

"Yeah, my date. He's stuck in traffic."

"Not a boyfriend, then?"

I give him a look, then a sharper one at his Budweiser bottle, playing like he's beneath me.

"He'll be here any moment. Weather, y'know."

"Probably a good idea not to have him pick you up at your place."

"Oh?"

"He would've had to take you, there and then, just inside the door. Lift that skirt and slip in deep and true."

Just like one of our dates back in ancient times. I abstain from picking up my martini because my hand will shake all that precious alcohol onto the bar.

"I already told you there'd be no funny business, Grant. It's just too complicated."

"But you're not denying that it's crossed your mind."

"Hard not to. Sex was never an issue between us. You're still reasonably attractive, and I'm not dead."

If anything, he's become hotter in the last year. Perhaps it's the slight sadness I imagine in his eyes whenever we meet. Melancholy shouldn't be so sexy.

"So the only thing in the way is a boatload of history, recrimination, bitterness, and failure." He sips his beer, a knowing lift to his eyebrow, all while keeping his eyes on me. "Just reasonably attractive, Bean?"

I shake my head. "Confidence was never your problem, Georgia."

"Oh, I don't know. I lost a little faith at one point."

And there it is again, that wall between us that's impossible to scale.

"Is this the point where I should apologize?"

"No," he says immediately. "I'm not saying that to make you feel guilty, simply telling you where I'm coming from. We know each other too well to sugarcoat it."

He's right. But our familiarity with each other's quirks and tics doesn't make it any easier. If anything, it's a millstone around our necks. We had something wonderful and it burned to an ash of regrets.

The sound of Elvis Presley's "*Burning Love*" interrupts the weighted silence between us. Grant removes his phone from his pocket and without even looking at it says, "I need to get this."

So much for having a moment.

He moves away a few feet but not before I hear his greeting to whoever's on the other end of the line. "Hey, sweetheart, I was hoping you'd call."

Hey, sweetheart?

My heart shrivels at the thought of Grant speaking to another woman with such obvious affection. It can't be his mother, so it must be—oh, God, maybe he's with someone. Wouldn't he have said?

Who knows? He's not mine anymore. I took care of that.

Less than sixty seconds—each of them nails into the cross of my heart—and he turns to me.

I stand, smoothing out my skirt. When I glance up, he's watching me with intent. "I'm calling it a night."

"Let's get something to eat."

"What happened to screwing ourselves stupid in your hotel room?"

"Baby, we'll need sustenance. You remember how it was."

I'd meant it as a joke, but of course Grant never joked about sex. He took it very seriously, and even though his initial comment was light, I know he's thinking of our marathons between the sheets. Hot, sweaty, slow burns that lasted long into the night.

But *hey, sweetheart,* right?

"Night, Grant."

And then I leave him, knowing his eyes are glued to my very fine ass.

~

BACK IN MY HOTEL ROOM, Cat Damon hisses at me for leaving him for so long, so I spend a few moments comforting him. Once he's settled, I pick up my work where I left off: a slideshow presentation I'm making to celebrate Libby's life. It's pretty much done but I'm nit-picking, moving images a pixel here and shaving off a second there.

Bored by my perfectionist self, I call Charlie, but she doesn't pick up. Probably banging her new husband. Next, I punch up Trinity, only to get a deep, male, British voice.

"Well, hello there, caller. Open your heart to your old mate Lucas."

"I'm looking for your woman."

"She's in the shower. I saw your name pop up and I figured it was an emergency."

"Don't be ridiculous, Wright. I'm just calling to gab with a girlfriend."

He remains silent, which I'm sure must be killing him because he's the chattiest person I know. Weirdly, Lucas has been a good friend to me in the last couple of months. After the divorce, my bond with Max became strained—he tried to be neutral but Grant and he work together so it was always going to be touch and go.

Lucas is close to both of them but he still manages to rise above the fray and somehow I've benefited with his broad shoulder. Don't mistake me, I have never cried in his presence (good God, he'd never let me live it down), but I have confided in him more than I would ever have done with a girlfriend.

"This was a terrible idea," I gush out. "I'm trying to have a quiet drink in the hotel bar and he shows up looking sexy as fuck."

"How dare he."

"Oh, shut up. Is he dating someone?"

"Not as far as I know."

I mull this over. Maybe it was his mom or his sister. "I haven't spent this much time with him in years and it's really weird."

"In a bad way?"

"Yes. And no." I sigh, running a hand along Cat's spine. He arches his back, begging for the good stuff. "It's just that sex would be a terrible idea."

"Why, because you'd want to get back together?"

"No, because it might give him hope."

He chuckles.

"What's so funny?"

"You, not putting out so as to not hurt his feelings. You're a martyr to the sanctity of divorce."

I give in. "Okay, so I don't want to get hurt. Grant has this way of—"

"Doing you?"

"Yes! He's Mr. Intensity, all super-focused, and it'll take me back to when everything was good and we felt invincible."

He hums. "Nostalgia can be a real drag. But maybe you should just try to focus on what was good about you two together and compartmentalize what was terrible."

"Easier said than done."

A text message pops in from Grant, a photo of what looks like my fantasy. In Cleveland.

It's a double burger, piled high with mushrooms and bacon.

The accompanying message: *This is happening.*

"Grant just sent me a picture of a hamburger."

"Boy's pulling out the big guns."

"He knows I love to fill my mouth with hot beef."

Lucas groans, which makes me giggle. Yeah, it was pretty bad, but it lightens my mood.

"Look, Aubs, I know you're hurting and you don't have to tell me why because the reasons are less important than the feeling. But you're in control of what happens to you. Even with top-notch burgers in the mix."

There's a bit of a scuffle, then what sounds like a few choice words. The next voice is Trinity's.

"Aubrey? Is everything okay?"

"Yeah, just checking in from beautiful snowy Cleveland. Your boyfriend's been giving me scary insight into the male psyche. His own."

"Oh, shit, no."

I laugh. "He's fine. I'm just feeling a bit raw, I suppose. Time with Grant does that."

"Well, I'm happy to stay on the line if it keeps you out of trouble." She lowers her voice. "But a little trouble might be good for you."

"Already told her that," Lucas chimes in.

"Men. Think they know everything."

I laugh. They're too cute together. "Off you go and do your thing."

I hang up, contemplating my next move. The hamburger gauntlet has been thrown down. Am I woman enough to pick it up?

CHAPTER 10

Grant

It takes ten minutes but finally I hear the knock. I'm not ashamed to say I do a little boogie right here in front of the door. Then, with renewed gravitas, I open up while executing a cool lean against the doorframe.

"'Sup."

Aubrey rolls her eyes affectionately. A faded gray hoodie with Northwestern Law emblazoned across it in purple falls off one too-thin shoulder. Her hair is piled high on her head and those sharp glasses of hers are perched on her nose. She probably thinks she's made herself less sexy. She would be wrong.

"Well, let's get this over with," she mutters impatiently.

I hold back the door and she passes by, careful not to touch me. Her mouth drops open at the sight before her.

"You—you ate my burger?"

"I ate *my* burger."

"But what the hell was that text all about?"

I pour a glass of Pinot, then hand it off before picking up

my beer. "I knew you wouldn't come over immediately because you wouldn't want to look too . . . oh, I don't know, *eager*. So I ordered one burger for myself and then—"

With perfect timing, a knock finishes my sentence.

"Hold that thought." I open the door to admit the room service guy who's shooting some healthy disdain my way for making him visit twice in thirty minutes.

"Your second order. Sir."

"Thanks, buddy." As he unloads the tray into the work desk, I sign the receipt, adding forty percent for the tip. Once he's gone, I unveil the tray. A steaming hot, fresh off the grill double burger with mushrooms and bacon awaits, complete with fries and all the fixings.

Aubrey stares at it, then me. "You were so sure I'd show?"

"No. But if you hadn't I would have delivered this to you myself. Ding, dong, ditch the burger."

She smiles. Worlds form and implode with that smile. "You're impossible."

"Just prepared. Get comfortable on the bed, Bean, and let me . . . do this." I was going to say "let me take care of you" like I used to, but it's too soon.

She growls, but does as she's told, a familiar ritual where she loads up on pillows and gets under the covers and waits for me to bring her treats. Candy or burgers or me.

I sit against the one pillow she's left for me (so greedy), with the tray in between us. She sips from her wine, eyeing me over the lip of the glass, then takes a fry. A tentative nibble, a serious chomp, followed by a pitch-perfect moment when joy lights up her eyes. I treasure it, just as I treasure every second with her. The good and the bad.

"Tell the truth," she says when she swallows.

"Always."

"You shook that fine ass when you heard my knock."

I feel a blush overtake me. "Ya got me, Bean." When we

first started dating, I used to dance my victory after every kiss, every touch, every smile. Sometimes in her presence, sometimes not.

She drops a light punch on my arm. "You haven't changed a bit since I met you. Still the guy who celebrates everything." She looks embarrassed at her pronouncement and returns to her burger, halving it with the steak knife, then picking it up and taking a big bite. We sit in silence for a while, me stealing fries, the overdone ones I know she doesn't like. We're a good team.

"I haven't eaten anything this good in forever."

She's clearly dropped a few pounds in the last year. I worry about her, but mentioning it will set her off. Eggshells dot the landscape around us.

"Done?"

She nods and I remove the tray to the desk. Back on the bed I offer her more wine, to which she shakes her head. Her frown tells me what's coming next.

"I should get back to my room."

"Before your foot rub?"

Her mouth twitches in appreciation. "I'm not sleeping with you."

"You haven't had the foot rub yet."

She swats at my chest, lets her fingers linger there. "Still work out?"

"Swimming. At Max's place." After Aubrey I started eating my feelings and not exercising, but I'm back in the best shape I've been in years.

Her fingers trace my shoulder, checking out my strong muscles. Her touch is divine, but I try my damnedest not to let her know how much she affects me.

"Lucas thinks I should go for it," she whispers.

"Go for what?"

"You. Use you and abuse you. These shoulders just might send me over to the dark side."

My pulse jumps, torn between the fact she's even contemplating using my body and that my friend and co-worker is somehow in the mix. "You talked about me to Lucas?" *I* don't even talk about me to Lucas.

"I was calling Trinity and he answered. You know how he is, won't shut up, has an opinion on anything."

I do. I love the guy but sometimes I want to punch him. Okay, most of the time.

Sipping her wine, she still watches me with those silver-gray eyes that see everything. "Maybe we should watch TV? While I think about the shoulders."

We could watch some god-awful reality show if she wanted, but I'm not liking how we're dancing around each other here. Like neither of us can settle.

"Sure, TV it is."

She picks a mob flick, something gory. Aubrey has always had a bloodthirsty streak. We stay a foot apart, though I'm aware of everything. Her shallow breaths, soft sighs, the way she flexes her toes. She's wearing socks but I'm mesmerized by her feet and it isn't long before she notices.

"Quit it, weirdo."

"Can't help it. Been a while since the object of my obsession has been so close."

"All right, make the most of it." She switches positions so her feet are in my lap.

I take full advantage, peeling off a sock. Slowly. Her feet are tiny, my hands are large, and the contrast has always added to our dynamic. I'm big and brutish, she's small and dainty. I could break her, except she got there first.

I drag my thumb along the arch of her foot, pushing in at certain points I know will make her feel good. She lets loose a whimper, then a strangled moan.

"Don't keep it in, Bean."

"Not that good yet."

It's torture to touch her like this, to be so close and yet still unsure of my welcome. I almost prefer watching her in the courtroom, where she manifests a frosty aloofness that keeps us both safe. Seeing Aubrey like this—touching her, yet not reaching her—is a battle I'm not sure I can win.

I renew my efforts to hear her moan. I'm a masochist of the highest order.

"Oh, that's it." She shimmies her body, stretching like a lazy cat. Which reminds me . . .

"Where's the demon?"

"Cat is asleep on my bed after a meal of tuna and spring veggies."

"So you're here because your room stinks."

She smirks. "Just do your job."

I do. She moans. I turn hard. The circle of life.

She stretches out her legs and positions her head on the pillow, looking up at me. "Thanks for doing this. I mean driving me home. I'm sorry I haven't said that already. I know this is the last place you want to be."

"I don't know. Cleveland has its charms." I'm looking at one of them.

"Still, it's super nice of you."

"Vibrator-induced dislocation?"

She blinks. "Excuse me?"

"Your injury." She'll have to tell me soon.

"I should get back," she says, though she makes no effort to leave.

"Worried you can't resist me?"

She rolls her eyes. "You've always been so damn cocky, Grant Roosevelt Lincoln."

"And you were never cocky enough."

Her brow furrows. "What does that mean?"

"You never had enough belief in your talents. In your awesomeness. You still don't."

"Belief isn't enough. I've always had to work harder than you. I might look the part, but the smarts never came naturally. You walk into the bar exam without opening a book. Me? I have to cram for four weeks of sleepless nights."

I shake my head. "Because you thought anything less than a hundred percent was a failure. Like you gave up cooking because your first couple of efforts didn't work out."

"I burned that lasagna."

"And the beef Wellington, which was kind of ambitious for someone who can't boil an egg."

"I wanted the first meal in our new place to be perfect."

I smile. "It already was. You were there."

"Grant, I—"

"All I'm saying is that you've always held yourself to this impossibly high standard, and as a result it's held you back."

She bolts upright. "There's nothing wrong with having standards. With wanting things to go right. Because when they go wrong, that's the worst feeling in the world, Grant."

"I know."

Her expression is one of torment, such that it kills me to have put it there. To bring up all these feelings again. That I might have made a huge mistake inserting myself into this journey gnaws at my chest. But it's *our* journey. We should travel it together.

She swings her legs off the bed. "Thanks for the burger. I should really . . ." She waves at the door.

"Coward."

Her eyes widen at my accusation. "What?"

"The second the conversation gets close, you clam up."

"You don't think we've talked enough? We have, Grant. We're both divorce lawyers and we can outtalk, out-argue, out-hurt each other better than anyone. And I know what it comes back to every time—my need to keep calm and carry on versus your compulsion to fix everything, including me. *Especially* me, who's basically not fixable. It was never supposed to work. We're too different."

"Yet it did for seven years. We made it work for seven years."

"Fought like cats and dogs the whole time."

I stand and face her, stare her down. "We always came back to each other."

Her eyes are huge, filled with passion. "With sex."

"With knowledge. Of who we are, of how we worked together, of the foundation we'd built. It shouldn't have been so easy to tear it down."

"Yet here we are."

I cup her jaw, giving her time to move away. "Here we are."

"I-I'm a mess, Grant." She waves a hand over her body as if her appearance is a problem for this. As if anything she could say would scare me away.

But I did run, once. And maybe that's why we're here. I should have fought harder.

"You think you're a mess? Not as much as you could be, Bean. Not as much as me." I kiss her, with the goal to turn her into the quivering puddle she's made of me.

Her mouth is so sweet, so responsive. I've missed it and all the honey that goes with it. The hunger and the joy.

Our tongues tangle, a perfect homecoming, a recognition of how goddamned good we are together. She moans into my mouth and I can't help it—I grasp her ass and pull her close, determined not to let her go.

But the move is too sudden. She pulls away, her eyes glazed. "This—I'm not sure I can do this."

I nod and somehow manage to separate my body from

hers. It feels so unnatural, but I try to cover. "You taste the same."

She touches her lower lip and darts her tongue over it, savoring me, I hope.

I grab a pillow and place it over my groin. "Don't do that. It's too much."

She smiles that cat's smile, and strangely it lightens the tension between us. I want her to feel in control, that she need never be concerned I'd push her too hard.

"Really?" She drags her teeth against her lip, leaving it wet and me wanting. Oh, she knows exactly what she's doing.

"Descendant from Salem witches. Knew it."

"I should leave." I think that's the third time she's said it but she can't follow through.

"Stay. But only if you can behave." I move back on the bed and stretch out with pillows at my back and my arm behind my head, inviting her in. "I'm not going to kiss you again. Not even if you beg me." I find the remote and flip around the channels until I find something I want to watch. *The Good Place,* which I like because Ted Danson is a genius.

She waits a beat, then another. After what seems like an eternity, she stretches out beside me. Not touching, but close enough to let hope take root in my chest.

CHAPTER 11

Aubrey

I wake in my ex-husband's arms and use the moment to truly look at him.

When I first met Grant, I couldn't believe how attracted I was to him. The notion of chemistry was abstract to me. Sure, I'd experienced lust, but never had I reacted so full-on to another person. I've always been suspicious of it. It's the New Englander in me. There's something both impractical and unseemly about letting your hormones overwhelm common sense.

In the early days, I used to sit behind him in class, ogling him, safe in the knowledge I could do so unobserved. He was the only person without a laptop, instead choosing to scrawl big florid loops on a legal pad. While everyone click-clacked away, he listened intently and made a note every few minutes. Watching him was a quiet revelation.

Now I try to assess with the eye of someone seeing this specimen for the first time. What is it about Grant that makes him so irresistible?

The physical attributes are undeniable, of course. The jaw is a thing of beauty. Strong and square, the perfect shelter for my forehead.

His lips are firm and giving. They've never disappointed.

But with Grant, it's always been his eyes. Dark blue, intense and fiery, yet heartbreakingly kind.

Right now, they're shuttered, thank God. To look into those eyes is to fall into madness. That's how it was when I first met him. My body was no longer my own—it fell over itself to become the property of Grant Roosevelt Lincoln.

I'm not so sure I ever held this same power over him. Sure, he enjoyed me, but with Grant, I suspect he enjoyed the conquest more. He got a kick out of my supposed Boston blue blood genes and how, in his view, I was slumming it with Bo or Luke Duke. We played that game for much of our time together, though it was likely more me trying to keep a layer of distance between us.

Grant needs something to grip, a reason to hope. He's a font of low-key yet boundless optimism, caged in six feet two of southern sexy gentleman. But there's steel in his gut. I've never met anyone more determined.

Which is why I said no to his offer of marriage the first time of asking.

Two weeks before graduation, I was still mulling my job situation. My father wanted me to come back to Boston and work in the legal department of the family firm. But Grant was staying in Chicago. He had an offer from Fairfax and Mullen, one of the top firms in the city. My Chicago offer was with a smaller, boutique outfit, which is what you got when your grades weren't so good.

Grant never doubted that we would follow the expected path: marriage after graduation, settle in the suburbs, pop out three children (two boys, one girl, per Grant). But then he was always the most assured person I'd ever met.

So when he asked me, I wondered if I could ever be as sure as him. Did I want to be that person? The daughter with the expectations heaped high, the fiancée with the going-places husband-to-be, the mother who wouldn't be able to find time for her kids, just like my own?

"I need to think about it."

Grant stared at me, from two feet below during a walk by the lake with the sun setting behind me (he'd dropped to one knee, of course), and then a sly smile curved his beautiful lips. "You never make it easy, do you, Bean?"

I wanted to scream that this wasn't one of our games. I wasn't trying to one-up him or make him work for it. I worried about being subsumed by his ambition. Grant had always known his journey. Was I just another trophy to be picked up on the way, another check in his inventory? But the words to explain it wouldn't form, so I tossed my head back and gave a coquettish laugh.

"Let's wait and see," I said.

I moved back to Boston.

Grant's response: *Taking this a bit far, aren't you, Bean?*

I told him I needed space. First year associates worked eighty-hour weeks, anyway. This time apart would help us figure it out.

For that first year, he came to see me in Boston every weekend, even if it was for one night only. I didn't think I could fall further than I already had but Grant Roosevelt Lincoln knew how to woo a girl. I was used to Cape Cod–wealthy frat boys, fast-talking investment bankers, guys with political ambitions constantly placed in my path by my constantly disappointed mother.

Grant was so different. Slow and deliberate in his speech, in his intentions, and between the sheets. He was a man on a mission and the mission was me.

He succeeded. I moved back to Chicago after a year and

we eloped to Vegas to get married. I couldn't bear the thought of my mother looking down on him or his lovely family during a big Boston wedding. She'd already made enough snide comments about his accent (*goes well with banjo music*), his considered approach (*whatever is he thinking in that southern-fried brain?*), and his smirk when presented with three forks and two spoons at her dinner table (*Grant, mon cher, use whatever catches your fancy*). My brothers saw him as some sort of carnival freak, even though he could run rings around them on any topic. And my father . . . well, Dad was usually three sheets to the wind whenever he was at home. Whenever he came home. His office sofa or between a (female) assistant's thighs had always held more appeal.

The only person who seemed to appreciate Grant as much as I did was my grandmother. I expected she'd tear him apart but he had a way with her. Made her feel beautiful with that Georgian charm. If Grant went missing during a home visit, I'd invariably find him with Libby in her granny flat (really a spacious apartment on the family estate—you'll see). Witnessing the two of them together, yukking it up, made my heart swell to epic proportions.

It would hurt her so much to know Grant isn't looking after me anymore. I know he can make it sound right if he talks to her in person. Well, not "sound right," because it can never sound right. No more Grant and Aubrey. It's the worst equation in the world, but Grant can spin it to acceptability. That's the best I can hope for.

Right now, lying beside him in a hotel room in Cleveland, I note that his breathing is steady, just like him. I've never felt safer with anyone than I do with Grant. His shirt has risen up a few inches, revealing taut muscle that my fingers sizzle with the need to touch. I trace an arrow of hair over his navel until my finger meets the barrier of his jeans, the first barrier of many. A button, a zipper, my hurt, and common sense telling me I shouldn't even think it.

Well, I've thought it and . . . I like it. I like it a lot.

I pop that button out of its mooring, then lift my gaze to his face.

Heavy-lidded eyes are watching me, alight with mischief. "Can I help you?"

"No." *Yes. This will help. This will help me feel in control, to just plain feel.*

My hand coasts across his abs, now that I have permission—wait, do I have permission? I stop, suddenly unsure. "Is —is this okay?"

He nods, and now it's his turn to look unsure. Or . . . gut-punched. As if my touch has knocked the wind out of him.

"Say it," I grind out. "I need a yes."

"Yes, Aubrey. I want you to touch me. I want you to do whatever the hell you need to me."

Not want, but *need*. No one can read me like this man.

Next comes the zipper, a slow, sexy slide down with some resistance from the bulge behind it. Maybe he's been hard all night. Maybe he's been hard since Chicago.

I brush my palm over his erection, straining against his black briefs. He lifts off the bed a couple of inches, arching into my touch.

"Tease," he murmurs.

"Easy," I murmur back.

"You think it's an insult, but where you're concerned, I wear it with pride."

I cup him and squeeze, my eyes never leaving his face. Oh, that's nice. The weight of him in my hand, the moan he lets loose, the crumple of his handsome face into pain/pleasure—it fuels my desire to a raging fire.

"Aubrey, I—I need to . . . need to touch you. Please."

"No, not yet." *Not ever.* Staying in control is my mission

here. If I let him touch me, slide his fingers inside my panties, rub through all the wetness he's created in me, I will no longer be in control here. And dammit, that's what I need. Just a measure of power, a grip over the life I can't keep inside the rails.

Giving my ex-husband a hand job might seem a strange way to get my mojo back. I can't explain it. I can only feel it.

"Jeans down," I order. When he doesn't do it immediately, I palm him harder.

On a lusty groan, he jerks his jeans and briefs down, and I'm left in awe of his beauty.

"Well, look at you," I say to his penis.

"You could look at my face."

"Much prefer to look at your cock." I run a finger along the underside, then wrap my hand around it. It's so thick I could weep for joy.

"Bean. Jesus." His abdominals flex like they're speaking to me and what they're saying is: *more more more*. A pearl of pre-cum leaks from the head and I can't resist: I swipe my tongue over it and taste.

"Oh, Christ," he says, before his hand cups my neck. "Sorry, can I? Please?"

Look at us, so careful with each other. The feel of him curled around my neck sends blistering heat throughout my body, along spokes to every extremity. I've always loved when he tunneled his fingers in my hair as he fucked my mouth.

I think I'm going to love it again.

I take him inside, bathing him with my tongue, hollowing my cheeks to suck. He's careful not to grip my neck too hard but I know he needs more. I need it, too. Whoever thinks blow jobs are an act of submission isn't doing them right. In this moment, I am queen, my ruin reframed as a power grab.

When he spills on my tongue, I swallow him down, then

continue to suck where it's sensitive until I'm sure I've milked him dry.

"Fuuuuck! Aubrey!"

I pull away and lay my head on his stomach. I can't look at him. Not yet.

His fingers massage the nape of my neck. "Still got it."

He means us, the undeniable sexual chemistry that makes us work. I shift my head so my chin's on his rock-hard abs and peek up at him through the veil of my lashes. "Queen of the Blow Jobs, remember?" Title earned on our fifth date.

"I need to catch up."

I bolt upright. "No."

"No?"

"You don't owe me an orgasm, Grant."

"Correct. I owe you three. At least."

My core flutters at the thought. He could do it, too. But I want to keep this other, new feeling close to my chest for a while.

"I'm going back to my room now."

He pulls a face, clearly baffled by my statement, which is downright adorable. "You sure?"

My heart feels lighter, even if every other part of me feels heavy with lust. If I can control this, I can get through the next few days. I'm sure of it.

"Let me walk you back," he says, evidently exasperated on realizing I won't bow down to his orgasm-producing skills.

"It's three doors down the corridor."

He stands, tucking himself back into his briefs and pulling up the zipper of his jeans. "A lot of unsavory characters in these parts."

I snort-giggle, and let him walk me back to my room.

"Thanks for the burger."

"Thanks for the blow job." He adds a cheeky grin that makes me melt, but I feel his unease at leaving me hanging.

Grant is a southern gentleman, not least in ensuring no woman is left behind.

Stay on target. "See you in the morning."

"Night, Bean."

GRANT INSISTS we go to the Rock & Roll Hall of Fame, and I have to give him this because he's being so nice to drive me. I even come inside and *ooh* and *aah* at the displays to prove I'm a good sport.

On the road to our proposed lunch stop in Erie, Pennsylvania, I get a call from my father. As his preferred methods of communication are all caps texting, incorrect emoji usage, and exclamation points, I answer immediately, worried about my grandmother.

"Dad, is everything okay?"

"Of course it is. Why wouldn't it be?'

I slide a glance to Grant, who is silently judging from the driver's seat. "I just thought—never mind. What's up?"

"Does something need to be up to call my girl?" His voice is loud and full of his usual bluster. I wish I'd waited until we'd stopped and I have more privacy.

"No, just surprised to hear from you. I'll be in Boston tomorrow."

"So, your mother is demanding the house in St. Bart's." The statement might sound like a non sequitur, but I know better. Never one to dwell on small talk, my father invariably steers our conversations to the divorce proceedings that could rival the decades-old case in Dickens's *Bleak House* for interminability. "She shouldn't be able to have a claim on that, should she?"

"You need to talk to your lawyer about it, but essentially

any property acquired during the marriage is fair game. You bought that less than ten years ago—"

He cuts me off. "With my money!"

"The courts don't really see it that way. There's more to a marriage than who paid for what. It's also about contributions, not all of them monetary. Mom kept the home fires burning while you"—*inserted your penis in strange women*—"ran a business." I've explained this to him several times, without the penis commentary.

"Surprised you'd take her side. She's never been the most maternal of women."

Who could blame her? I certainly don't.

Let me tell you more about the Gates of Boston, one of the oldest and most elite families in New England. Some species of birds, like cuckoos, are what's known as brood parasites. They lay eggs in the nests of other birds, sometimes killing off the host's young, and fool the host into bringing up the baby birds as their own. My life is a human version of this.

Dad had an affair and I was the result, inherited by the Gates family when my biological mother died after birth complications. I don't know why he and his wife remained together, but somehow Marie-Claire was convinced to adopt me. The family knows about his mistake—which somehow has morphed into mine—but we don't talk about it. We just carry on as if bringing home the child of your dead mistress and expecting your wife to raise her is perfectly normal.

Marie-Claire is the only mother I've ever known. She can't help her chilliness toward me. Hell, I understand it. All my life, I've tried to demonstrate appropriate gratitude because I was taken in, a cuckoo's egg in the host nest. And my father now likes to use my mother's good deed as ammunition in his war with her.

"I'm not taking sides, Dad. And I've told you I can't give

you advice on this. That's why you have very expensive divorce lawyers who specialize in Massachusetts divorce law." It's not all that different from anywhere else, but my father is awed enough by legalese that it momentarily buys me an out.

"So how's Libby?" I ask. He has a contentious relationship with his mother, my grandmother. She does *not* approve of his life choices.

"High as a kite half the time."

"I can't wait to see her. And all of you," I quickly add.

Now that I'm no longer kowtowing to my father's ego, I'm quickly dispatched.

"Papa Gates sounds to be in fine form," Grant comments when I click off.

"Can it, Lincoln," I mutter, not in the mood.

We stop at a diner in Erie, where I order a chef's salad and Grant gets the grilled cheese with bacon. Tons of bacon, which I help myself to out of kindness to his arteries. He leans over and picks up my water glass, then salts the napkin. My heart gives a strange twist at this familiar gesture. He always did that so my glass wouldn't stick to the soggy napkin.

"Let's talk about last night," he says.

"Let's not."

"I'd like to know why you wouldn't let me reciprocate."

"Sheesh, most guys wouldn't even question it. Most guys would take it as their due."

He narrows that dark gaze at me.

"Yeah, I know, Grant. You're not most guys."

"This was never our dynamic. I don't like leaving you unsatisfied."

"Who says I was left unsatisfied? I can take responsibility for my own orgasms."

His cheekbones flag with color. Sometimes he's so easy,

but he turns it around in a flash because he's also quick. "That's the sound I heard through four walls?"

"You did not—" I break off, realizing he's kidding. "I'm just saying that what happened was something I needed. It's been a while since I've felt . . . well, sexual. And being in charge of your pleasure gave me a sense of control."

He stares at me for an electric moment, no doubt surprised by my admission. I'm a little surprised myself.

"And if I'd touched you, if I'd run my fingers through your slickness, inside, you might have lost that?"

Now it's my turn to heat up. "I'm not ready to hand that over just yet. And when I do, I don't know if it will be with you."

Instead of being insulted, he grins and my heart twists the other way. "Ah, so you're just practicing on me while you get your groove back?"

"What's wrong with that?"

"Wicked, wicked woman."

And here we are grinning at each other like fools, wondering how it could have ever gone wrong.

About halfway through our meal, I hear voices alternating between agitated and soothing, and notice several diners around us rubbernecking to a point behind me. What looks like the manager is at a booth over in the corner. His back is to us but I can just about see who he's talking to: a woman.

Correction: a woman with a baby. The child wails and the man recoils as if the sound offends him. Which is when I see what truly offends him.

She's breastfeeding—or was. Her shirt is open to the navel but pulled closed, like hastily drawn curtains over what should be a natural sight. My eyes dart around, looking for the asshole who probably complained and started this mess.

Now that we're listening, snatches of what they say reach us:

"Got no right . . ."

"Restroom . . . over there . . ."

"Leave her be . . ."

Then me to Grant, as I'm barely able to see through my red-eyed rage: "Be right back.

"Hello," I say, muscling in, though I don't really have the presence or the power suit to make it work. "We're all dying to know what's happening over here."

"Ma'am, please go back to your meal," the manager says, oily as margarine, "I'm sorry you were disturbed."

"Oh, I wasn't." I turn to the mom. She's so young and looks so tired. The woman across from her in the booth is an older version of her, possibly her own mother.

As for the baby . . . oh, he's got a ton of dark hair and piercing blue eyes. "Boy or girl?"

"A boy. Simon." She looks wary, no doubt questioning if I'm here to pile on the litany of complaints.

"How old's Simon?" I take a seat at the edge of the booth to let her know I'm an ally.

"Six weeks. Six weeks tomorrow."

I reach to touch his head, then stop myself.

"Oh, go on," the woman says. "He's a bit cranky because he's hungry"—she arrows an accusing look at the manager, who is now standing awkwardly, peering down at three women, which is *never* a good look—"but he doesn't bite."

I graze my knuckles gently over his cheek. He's surprisingly warm and that newborn scent hits me so hard my ice-compacted heart cracks open.

"Did this gentleman tell you that you couldn't breastfeed here?"

"He said we have to use the restroom, but it's filthy and no place to feed a child," the other woman cuts in. She offers her hand. "I'm Carrie Ann. This is my daughter Bailey."

I shake it. "Hi, ladies. I'm Aubrey and I'm a lawyer. I practice family law in Chicago but I'm fully versant in the regulations in this state. All women have the right to breastfeed their children in public."

The manager coughs. "We had a complaint—"

"And when faced with the choice between acknowledging a complaint and breaking the law, you chose the latter?" I tut, which makes Carrie Ann laugh and the manager turn an ugly shade of red.

"I have to take all my customers into account," he sputters.

My phone vibrates and I remove it from my pocket to find a text from Grant with the exact Pennsylvania Consolidated Statute number and a link, just in case I need to wow with the full force of the law. My heart does a few rabbit kicks.

"I think the local news and area women's groups would be very interested to interview you"—I squint at his name tag —"*Jacob*. Or maybe I'll check in on Facebook and see if we can get this thing going viral."

He raises his hands. "No, no, of course she can do . . . that." Without so much as an apology he backs away.

"Wow," Bailey says, with a nervous grin, "you sure told him."

"I can't stand bullies." My gaze is drawn back to the baby, this gorgeous bundle of life and joy. "And I'm a sucker for cutie pies."

Now that the confrontation is over, my thigh starts to shake. Maybe it's adrenaline—it's not, it's not—but I'm suddenly feeling dizzy. Which means it's a good idea to stand, right?

Ha, of course it is! I grip the table as I lever myself up one-handed.

"Well, enjoy the rest of your meal. Especially, you, little

one." My voice must sound strange because both women scrunch up their faces at me.

They say something, probably thanks, but there's a rushing sound in my ears, a waterfall thundering through my brain. My heart thumps, thumps, thumps, and I back away, pivot quickly, and stumble blindly toward the restroom.

CHAPTER 12

Grant

I shouldn't follow her, but I can't let her cry alone. Too much of the time managing our grief was spent in separate rooms.

"Bean."

She wipes her eyes and turns away from me to blow her nose. "You can't be in here."

I flip the lock behind me. "Yet I am."

She shakes her head. "God, I hate when assholes like that stick their oar in. Just who the hell did that guy think he was?" She goes on in this vein for a while, and after about thirty seconds, I take her into my arms.

"Grant—"

"Can I hold you, Bean?"

"I'm okay." She sniffs. "I was doing so well. It's been months since I lost it and I need to pull it together before we get to Boston."

"It's okay to get upset. I don't think you ever realized that."

Drawing back, she stares at me, her eyes puffy and swollen. "Thanks for giving me permission."

Irritation flares. "Well, you always acted like you needed it. Like any deviation from the stiff upper lip would be punished to the full extent of your mother's law."

She tries to draw back. I hold on, like I should have two years ago.

"You had a miscarriage, Aubrey. You lost a child you had already started to love, and you—you refused to talk about it."

"You know that's not how I was brought up."

"So staying trapped in that cycle of your upbringing is the only way forward?"

She pulls away from me, and this time I let her because, no matter how much I try, I can't make her melt into me.

"It got me through."

"It got you out."

She places a finger of accusation in my chest. "Here we go. I won't beat my breast and wail my grief in a way that suits Grant Roosevelt Lincoln."

I shake my head, gaping at her capacity to reframe the narrative. "You wanted to grieve alone. I thought it should be a joint effort."

"What's wrong with my way? Why does everything have to be hashed out, talked about, pored over, until we're hoarse? Why couldn't we just move on? Oh, right, you did. When you said you couldn't live with me anymore. You couldn't . . . love me anymore."

A single tear escapes, and before she can swipe it away, I catch it with my thumb. I cup her head and lean in close.

"I never said I couldn't love you anymore, Bean. I wanted us to talk, go to counseling, figure out a way to grieve that acknowledged our pain. Our. Pain. This didn't just happen to you. I know you went through indescribable hurt, baby. But when you wouldn't let me in, I felt like you didn't need me anymore."

The moment it leaves my mouth, I realize that this is the story of my life. My mother, pregnant at fifteen by an older man who wouldn't acknowledge what he'd done, disowned by her parents, forced to find her own way, raised me alone. The moment I could get a job, I started paying her back, becoming the knight she needed. Every decision I made from school to work to my choice of bride has been to make my momma proud and create a life that says "fuck you" to everyone who said we couldn't. I know I chose Aubrey for a reason.

She needed me.

On first glance at our upbringing and obvious differences, this sounds like crazy talk. Why would a woman with Aubrey's privilege and advantages want to slum around with a guy from the backwoods? What could I possibly offer her? But that first day we met I saw it all laid out as clear as a Chicago summer sky: I would show her the meaning of worship and in turn she would give me purpose. I would craft a perfect life with her, shelter her and the family we would make. My silver-eyed, broken princess would be healed by my touch.

I'd already taken care of my momma, and every knight needs a new crusade.

"Of course I needed you," she says, "but what I mostly needed was to go back to our lives. To fighting and fucking, the way we do it. Grant and Aubrey. Instead you treated me like a glass doll. Like I was no longer a woman, just a fragile, broken vessel who couldn't—" She stops.

"Who couldn't what?"

"Carry the son and heir. Give you that dream you'd wanted. The whole nine."

I treated her like glass because that's what she was—*is*—to me. Precious. Mix that with my guilt at being unable to keep my rough, redneck hands off her. My worship was real but rarely reverent.

She closes her eyes, her black lashes dotted with diamond-shaped tears. "I felt . . . like such a failure. This thing you wanted, this life you needed . . . I couldn't give it to you. And you wanted to talk about it. About trying again. About how we could get through it. And all I could think of was . . ."

"What, Bean? Tell me."

"You'd be better off without me. With someone who could give you it all and wouldn't keep on hurting you."

Jesus. *Fuck fuck fuck*. How did she get to that? Was that the message I'd somehow instilled in her: *picket fence and two point five kids, or you're worthless to me*.

I'm so angry I can't think straight, or maybe I'm thinking straight for the first time in forever.

I release her and step back, my hurt that she would unilaterally decide our future by clamming up and pushing me away creating a rage-mist surrounding me. She's opening her heart and what's coming out should make me understand. At last.

Yet the thoughts in my head are all about me: *How dare she do this? How dare she make that call?*

"I guess you didn't know me at all."

She opens her eyes, clearly alarmed at the frigid tone of my words.

A wave of anger, guilt, and lust crashes over me, as inextricably linked as two people with a shared past and grief.

"Your job was never to provide an heir, Aubrey. Maybe that's what your family has drilled into you from day one, and I can't deny that I wanted kids. That the thought of you carrying my child excited me, made me giddy. I just wanted to care for you. Shelter you. Heal you. But that you'd use our loss to finish what we had, to call time on us—who the fuck do you think you are?"

Her eyes widen. Anger has never been one of my tools. I'm low-key to the point a stiff breeze might knock me over. But this . . . I'm caught between my own guilt and the need to make her understand that we were once a team and *she fucking ruined it.*

"Grant," she breathes, her hand fanning out over my chest. The touch of her burns and I crave it like a man dying to meet his maker. Because while my momma grew me from a seed, Aubrey shaped me into a tree. Fury is rocketing through me, and what's more, it's . . . it's turning me on.

"Grant," she says again as she cups my jaw and that . . . that . . . *that* incendiary touch breaks me wide open. I take her mouth, this mouth I adore, and crush it with all my dead hopes and dreams. With the need I can't muster for anyone else and the guilt I can no longer hide.

It's a bomb, this kiss. The shrapnel makes our hands tear at each other's clothes but I'm stronger and push her away. I don't deserve her touch. I don't deserve a damn thing. Yet I want to give her what she wouldn't permit last night. My hand inside her panties. My fingers invading her heat. All my want wrapped up and ready to detonate.

Pain is supposed to make you stronger, some idiot said. Love, too. With Aubrey, I feel nothing but fear and weakness, desire and longing. When do I reach the part about becoming a better person?

I plunge my fingers inside her, breaching her body, loving her sensual gasp. In this, we've always been able to find each other. When we couldn't communicate, our bodies did the heavy lifting.

She screams into my mouth as my rough-hewn fingers press against her clit. The jerk of her body is my gold medal, but in that moment, I feel as though I've stolen it. This gift she didn't want to bestow on me. This orgasm she wanted for her own.

Still clutching my shoulders, her forehead slots in under my chin. I clamp her tight, soothing her through the fall. My first instinct is to apologize, but she raises a finger to my lips before I can say the words.

"It's okay," she says, though it's not, and I'm not sure it ever will be.

Someone knocks on the door, breaking the noisy peace we found for one small moment.

Silently, we fix ourselves up and go on our way.

CHAPTER 13

Aubrey

I jolt awake to the sound of a cry. For a moment I think it's her.

No, it's Cat Damon. We must have hit a patch of ice. He's sensitive to any sudden movements of the car.

I look over to Grant, who is focused on the road. He asks, "You okay?"

"Yeah, I thought—where are we?" The sky is dark, which means I've slept since Erie. Bacon and Grant-given orgasms for the win.

"About an hour outside Skaneateles."

"The Finger Lakes? But I thought we were going to stop in Buffalo."

"Decided to press on."

So he can deliver me to Boston sooner and think of a way to dump me there, no doubt. A shiver runs through me. We've been here before—a different car, another road, at these lakes. Three times we've driven to Boston for the holidays and three times we've stopped in one of the towns in the Finger Lakes region. It's almost a tradition.

"Means we can sleep in tomorrow," he adds. "Shorter drive to the city."

This morning I woke up at 2 a.m. in Grant's arms. It felt right and wrong and everything in between. One take-back-my-power blow job later countered with a reciprocal orgasm after my diner meltdown, and here we are.

"Has he been whining while I slept?" I look back at Cat Damon, who eyes me with typical accusation.

"No more than usual."

"I think he misses you."

Grant snorts. They have a love-hate thing going on that I don't buy for a second.

By the time we get to Skaneateles, a pretty town hugging the shores of its namesake lake, it's close to dinnertime. I'd been hoping for a gray block of hotel on the highway; instead, I'm in a colonial mansion with so many festive wreaths, I'm drowning in Hallmark. Happy freakin' holidays.

"One room," I comment as we head up to the third floor, the walls framed with Victorian cameos and daguerreotypes that look authentic.

"Don't make a thing of it, Aubrey." No more "Bean," I see. His voice sounds as strained as the journey has felt over the hours since Erie. Since I fell apart in that restroom under his touch and told him we ended because I couldn't be the wife he needed.

Grant grabs the spare pillows and comforter out of the closet. He throws them on the sofa to let us all know what the sleeping arrangements will be tonight.

Okay, then.

Neither of us is hungry, and with the weather and our moods, I'm not seeing any romantic walks in our immediate future. At least a foot of snow, maybe more is expected.

I coax Cat Damon out of his carrier. "Come on, Cat."

He's upset with all the travel, so I let him wander the room sniffing things and rubbing against the furniture. I set out his bowl with some bottled water and open up cat food from a baggie, that dry junk that's supposed to be good for them.

"Okay if I use the bathroom first?" Grant asks.

"Sure!"

We're back to being careful around each other.

With him out of my presence, I breathe for the first time in hours. I've never seen Grant angry before—irked, annoyed, turned on, dominant, but never furious, not even when it was clear our marriage was failing. Back then, we skirted each other like ghosts passing from one realm into the next. Sadness was the primary emotion, waterlogging us for the countdown to the end.

An angry Grant is interesting. And hot.

I know he's hurting. I told him I'd given up on us because I assumed he was disappointed in my failure to give him a child. Maybe it was a cop-out. That time is a blur—a wave of pain and misery that even now I can't adequately elucidate the sharp, pointed whys and why-nots. What is it they say? Hurt people hurt people, and back then that's all we seemed to do.

One day a couple of years ago stands out, one when I thought we were finally getting somewhere. The front door to our home opening and closing sent a wave of panic through me. *My husband was home.*

"Aubrey?" Grant appeared at the entrance to the kitchen, his eyebrows raised quizzically. He put down his travel bag. "What's going on?"

What's not going on? The oven chose this perfect moment to beep . . . no, not the oven. The smoke alarm! My first instinct was to yank open the oven door where the roast I'd slaved away on all afternoon was cooking. And cooking.

Bad move. It just sent smoke billowing out into the kitchen.

Grant grabbed a dish towel and waved it below the smoke alarm, then flipped the switch on the circuit breaker. He placed his hands on his hips and gave me a pitying look.

"You're making dinner?"

I pinned a smile on my face. Cooking was not my forte, which I suspected was a disappointment to Grant, who had hoped for more from his wife.

"Don't sound so shocked. I wanted to surprise you." Meanwhile the surprise was burning to a crisp. With oven-gloved hands, I took out the tray and placed it on the counter. There was no resuscitating that mess.

"Damn, I thought I was being so careful."

He put an arm around me, and it felt strange enough for me to freeze up for a second. Sensing my reaction, he dropped his hand.

It had been two months since our world had cleaved in two. On one side of our union I lay, barely able to operate. On the other, my husband waited for me to become the woman he married. I didn't cook as a rule, so this was probably not the best way back into his heart, but I wanted to try something different. Something not hardwired in my brain as reflective of our new normal.

He picked up a steak knife and poked at it. "Dead as a doornail, Bean. Nice job."

"Oh, shut up." I tried to enjoy his teasing. "How was your trip?"

"Uneventful." He'd gone to New York to take a deposition from a client who couldn't come to Chicago. Frankly, the couple of days apart felt shockingly easy. Guilt wracked me at the thought I enjoyed this break from the man I loved more than anything. But it wasn't a break from Grant so much as a break from the *me* I was around him. Alternating between Ms. Mope and a desperate nymphomaniac. I wanted what we had and my husband insisted on treating me as if I'd just had a death in the family.

Which made him a good person and me a monster.

"Pizza it is, then," he said with a wicked smile, and in that moment, I thought: *we'll be fine*. "I'm going to take a shower. You okay calling it in?"

"It's the least I can do after messing up my romantic dinner plans."

His brow pleated at the mention of romantic dinners. That was usually Grant's job, and here I was usurping his authority in the arena of woo.

"Off you go!" I shooed him away.

Forty-five minutes later, and we were chomping on pizza, trying to pretend everything was the same as before it happened. As if we were just Grant and Aubrey, lawyer super couple, blessed and beloved.

I'd read everything there was about miscarriages and how I was supposed to react. The consensus was that there was none, but I still suspected I was getting it wrong and not following the grief playbook to the letter. What was hardest was the idea that I was at the mercy of my body and it had betrayed me.

It was my body's job to bring this being safely into the world, to be the vessel that carried him or her. And this body—this fragile, weak, corruptible mess of flesh—had failed.

Your mission, should you choose to accept it, is to not kill the baby lying inside you.

I wanted to get us back in sync, back to where I called the shots. Grant could help by treating me and my body the way he had before. I didn't want this sadness weighing me down.

Returning to the banality of before—where we fought and fucked and felt—was my new mission.

After pizza, we settled in to watch a movie and I exhaled in relief: we were back. And when my hand went to his chest as the movie credits rolled and slid further to the waistband of his sweatpants, it felt like the most natural thing in the world.

"Grant," I whispered against his neck as I cupped his half-hard cock.

"Bean." He took my hand and moved it up to his abs. Away from where I needed it and where I thought he needed it. We hadn't been intimate since the night of the miscarriage, when we'd had sex before going out to dinner. Me tempting Grant in that red dress he loved so much, him unable to resist.

Before everything changed.

Sensing my disappointment, he said, "Kind of tired. Long day on the road."

"Of course!" I offered a bright smile that affirmed I was okay. *We're okay. This is nothing more than a bump.*

Except he'd been tired the week before and didn't use travel as an excuse. As that thought wound around my brain, I decided, *screw this.*

"I can't help but get the impression you're just not that into me anymore, husband."

He shot up, visibly affronted. "What? That's crazy. I'm just tired. If anything . . ." He stopped.

"If anything . . ."

He swallowed. "If anything, I'd prefer we talked more about what happened, about how we feel before we go down that road."

"What is there to say? It happened, Grant. That's all there is to it."

"Really?" The word was shot through with disbelief. "You

don't have any feelings about it? Anything you want to share? About your pain, your grief, your loss?"

Why was it *my* pain, *my* grief, *my* loss? This notion that I needed to unburden here because my hurt supposedly had higher value than his offended me. This wasn't just my problem because the baby had once been tethered physically to me. Or maybe I was too annoyed with Grant's rejection to see what he really wanted: for us both to be honest.

My Yankee practicality rose with my ire. "Can't we just take the pain and grief as a given? Skip the steps and move on to the healing?" And what I meant was the sexual healing.

He looked at me like I was a frigid-hearted automaton, incapable of the minimum necessary to show true human feeling. But I felt numb and I suspected I would only feel *un*numb again if Grant stopped treating me with kid gloves.

"I'm trying to help here," he said with strained patience.

"There's only one way you can help, Grant, and it's not with your folksy southern charm."

His face became a mask then, a complete blank to my casual dismissal of his ability to use words, the weapons of his trade, to fix this. I didn't need long speeches about the baby that would never be born. I needed to be lusted after.

But it wouldn't be happening tonight. Exasperated, I stood, and went to our bedroom. Alone.

Months and years later, I realize that I did him wrong. I need to rectify that.

He comes out of the bathroom, wearing only sweats, and by God, my libido goes hello! I'm such a weakling for that thickset body. He walks over to the window and peers out.

"Storm's a rager," he mutters.

I don't like the sound of that. "We're going to be able to get out, aren't we?"

"Yeah, we'll be fine. Bathroom's free."

Prepared for supplication, I sit on the bed. Something has

to give and I'm starting to realize it needs to be me. "About what happened back at the diner?"

"Which part?"

"All of it. Back then—two years ago—I shut down. And you were so lovely to me, all the time. So gentle. And I didn't want that. I wanted the rough-and-tumble of teasing and fighting and battles in the courtroom, with sex our reward."

"Aubrey . . ." He rubs his mouth. "How could we just pretend it hadn't happened? Did you think we could just fuck our way back to normality?"

I lift a shoulder, overcome with my sheer stupidity. "Yeah, I-I did."

"Baby, that was never going to work, not when . . ."

"Not when what?"

He passes over my question. I feel as if I've missed something important, some insight into Grant's psyche, which has always been so focused on my pain and not his own.

"You didn't fail me," he says, though I think he wanted to say something else. "I know that's what you thought and I know I didn't handle it right. Telling you we could try again."

"It's something people say. The doctor said it."

"But it's not what you needed to hear, as though what we lost could be easily replaced."

Yes. That's what it sounded like. Like the baby we'd formed wasn't formed enough to love or protect or even mourn.

"We both made mistakes."

He nods, and then smiles tentatively as if trying it out. It's like sun after the storm, and I absorb it like a thirsty sponge.

"Better get some rest so we can head out early tomorrow and hit Boston around lunchtime."

"Okay." I get ready for bed, conscious that a half-naked man is stretched out on the sofa, which is really more of a love seat. His feet dangle over the armrest, the whole thing can barely contain him.

"Grant, you can sleep in the bed if you want to."

"Fine here."

"You'll never get any sleep on that sofa." I place a pillow to my left side, the separation we need. "Just get in, Georgia."

Resigned, he stands and rubs a hand over his chest. He used to do that a lot, not to tease or titillate, just a habit. Grant's always been a very tactile person. Not me—I can't even recall a hug from my mother or father that wasn't done under sufferance. We're not that kind of family.

At the side of the bed and with his back to me, he pulls down his sweatpants, and lo and behold, let us testify to the glory of Grant Roosevelt Lincoln's ass. The man has a perfectly sculpted form, beautiful rounds cupped lovingly by black cotton. All the parts of me that should be affected go into overdrive—my breasts, my stomach, my thighs, my feet. Yes, my feet! I am tingling everywhere.

Then there's his back, beautifully broad with bite-me muscles. He doesn't work out much, either. Just runs, and swims, apparently. And then the lovely vista is gone, replaced by another, his chest as he lies back, his arm behind his head. His pecs are lightly furred and my fingers develop an itch.

He catches me staring. "What?"

"Nothing." I turn off the light on my side of the bed.

In the dark, he switches on his e-reader. "Will this bother you?"

"No, not at all."

I've always liked to watch him read, and now is no different, like this is us and how we used to be. I pretend it's normal until sleep takes a hold of me.

CHAPTER 14

Grant

I wake up in a cold bed.

My hand moves to check the space to my right past the pillow barrier, where she should lie. Nothing.

I sit up, my heart thundering. This was common in the old days. She didn't want me to hold her unless it would lead to sex. I'd held too tight and cursed us.

But this night—this whole trip—is different. Something happened in that diner. We're not back to Grant and Aubrey, but we're somewhere different, a possibly useful detour.

I listen for sounds from the bathroom, but all I hear is the wind. Standing at the window, I peer out into the dark void, searching for movement and finding nothing. My heart is booming like a rocket around my chest.

Where is my wife?

A gentle thud grabs my attention, so I put my head around the bathroom door. The night-light gives it an ethereal glow, and lookie here, if it isn't the dumb cat standing on his hind legs in the sink, gazing at himself in the mirror. That pirate is so fucking weird. I imagine he's pumping himself up, telling his reflection he's the best cat there is and it doesn't matter what the other cats say.

"Hey, buddy, you okay?"

"M#%&*!"

I take a look in the mirror, trying to see what the cat does. All I get is me, this fucker I'm tired of. I'm not sure how I imagined this trip, but amazing blow jobs and angry sex in diner restrooms wasn't it. Will I have to shatter Aubrey into a million pieces before I can put her back together again? I don't have it in me to be cruel; hurting her is like lopping off one of my own limbs.

Cat makes a throaty-scratchy sound, so I pick him up and take a seat on the toilet.

"What ya think, Cat? Momma gone to raid the inn's kitchen?"

"M@*#$!"

"Yeah, I'm worried about her, too."

A sound makes me jump. Aubrey stands in the doorway of our room, her red coat and boots dusted with snow, her eyes bright with the cold. Snow White on a mission.

My relief at seeing her safe emerges raw from my throat. "Where the fuck have you been?"

"Shush. Not in front of Cat Damon." She comes in and shuts the door. "Couldn't sleep, so I took a walk."

"I woke up and you—shit, Aubrey, it's a storm out there." The cat jumps down, so I stalk over to Aubrey and go to unbutton her coat—then realize that it's already open, draped over her shoulders because of the sling, and the front of her sweatshirt is damp. Which meant she was outside in the snow with her coat open.

I pull that damn coat off her shoulders with a vengeance. "Don't do that, Aubrey. Just. Don't."

Her silver eyes spark in recognition. "Oh. You thought I was gone."

"Wouldn't be the first time."

"I came back."

She would walk around the garden at night or go for long drives after it happened. By then we were sleeping in separate rooms, so I'd stand at the window of the guest room, watching her circle the fish pond, waiting for the headlights to tell me she'd returned.

Tonight, her body is a block of slippery ice. I place my hands on her shoulders then roughly palm her upper arms.

"Grant," she says, but I ignore her, bent on my goal to make her warm. Make her whole. *Make her mine.*

"Grant," she repeats. "I'm okay. I just wanted to feel the storm, to absorb some of its crazy. My grandmother used to take me out in the middle of Nor'easters so I could experience true power."

I stop my vigorous rubdown. "You never told me that."

"Gotta keep some mystery, Georgia."

"You're freezing."

"I'm alive."

She is, her body thrumming, her eyes frost-bright with it. "I'm sorry. For everything I put you through. For all the hurt I caused you when I shut you out."

"Bean, you don't have to do this."

"I do. I need you to know that I was wrong. I know this half-assed apology doesn't make it right but—"

I cut off her half-assed apology with my mouth on hers, stamping it with all my need and want. Here she is giving me what I want to hear—absolving me of my sins—and I can't stand it. I can't stand for her to take on that blame.

Our mouths grind together in a sinuous slide of pent-up desire now blasted wide open. Shrapnel, shrapnel, everywhere. But I can take the blows because each one makes me feel alive again. I get what she means about the power of the storm. In truth, it's the power of us.

"Need—need to touch you," she gasps, her hands running point over my chest, mapping all the old haunts she used to love. I let her, then grip the hem of her sweatshirt.

She raises her hands in surrender and I help her remove the shirt, careful not to pull at her casted arm.

Bared to me at last.

She is as beautiful as the first moment I saw her. More so because she's been through so much and her goodness still shines through.

My hands, brain, and dick are on the same page: touch her everywhere. I've thought about this for years, how it would be when I get the full Aubrey experience again. I would run my hands over her pale body with reverence, let her know how much I appreciated every inch of her. I would take it slow.

Fuck that.

Like a wolf in heat, I grasp her ass and pull her into me, squeezing her plump flesh. No gentle workup, this is rough because that's what I am with Aubrey. I'm a beast.

"Missed this," she murmurs. "Missed you."

All I can do is growl and take her mouth again, thrusting my tongue while I grab ass like a grab-ass pro.

"Get on the bed."

"Make me," she shoots back.

Oh, it's on.

I push her onto the bed and push down my briefs. I'm so hard it hurts but I don't touch myself yet.

That honor will go to her.

Instead I take her left foot and pull off her boot and sock, then the other. Next the sweatpants, still damp from the storm. Outside it's raging, and inside it's going to get cat-five any minute.

She's spread out before me in those panties that look like shorts. I kneel in between her thighs, paralyzed by my desire for her. She's still this tiny, fragile thing and I want inside her so badly, but I worry I'll hurt her all over again.

She sits up on her elbows. "Grant, I need you." Her hand wraps around my cock, hard and ready for her, and I close my eyes to savor and shake.

Her next words are soft. "Has there been anyone else?"

My eyes blink open.

She bites her lip. "I mean, unprotected."

"The last woman I was with, protected or unprotected, was my wife."

That earns me a watery smile. "And the last dick that graced the halls of my vagina belonged to my husband."

I love her mouth. "Lucky guy."

"I always thought so."

Not just lucky, but blessed. Being chosen by Aubrey was the greatest thing to ever happen to me. I never thought I deserved her but I sure as hell wasn't going to give her up.

Until it hurt too much to hold on.

"And I'm on birth control. So nothing to—well, you know." That word "birth" sits up between us, but she rushes on. "Take what you need, Georgia."

She was never one to stand on ceremony. Never needed me to ease in, but I do because I need it to go slow. I need it to last because I suspect I'll be dining off this memory for a long time.

I notch at her entrance, nudging, watching the broad head slip inside. One inch. Two.

"Stop teasing, you prick," she mutters, whether to me or my dick I don't know. I laugh because this is my Aubrey, back from the dead.

The slide is crazy tight, crazy hot, as I fill her up. *Too good. Too good. Too fucking good.* I have been a zombie for two years. Only with her do I feel like a flesh-and-blood person.

Gripping the curve of her ass, I move inside her, taking care to keep her pinned in place where I can remain in control. For all Aubrey's smart talk, she loves when I lead like this. Her bossiness is an act, cultivated for the courtroom. When we're together, she's a kitten, letting me pet and stroke her, arching her back, murmuring desperate demands for more.

I give it to her, as hard as she needs it. The rhythm remains steady as I try to hold back, anxious not to overplay my hand. Sex with Aubrey has always been a test of my endurance, but this feels like a test of my humanity. I've been a ghost without her and now, with each thrust, parts of me reappear, as if from across some divide.

Stroke. Muscle, bone, and sinew returns.

Thrust. Skin covers my frame, binding me together.

Groan. Her nails dig into my ass and I feel more real than I have in two years.

She tightens around me, the quiver of her pussy the final step to my completion. My deadened heart beats again, pumping life into this shell I've lived in since we parted. Her scream as she comes triggers my release, which goes on and on, so long I'm sure I've set some sort of record.

I pull out as soon as my brain recognizes the risk of crushing her body with mine. Checking in with her, my gaze is drawn to her cast.

"How did this happen?"

"Well, you got all caveman about me being out in a snow-storm and then two seconds later we're going at it like the world is ending tomorrow."

I growl. "Talking about your arm."

"Oh, that." She shrugs and mutters something about feelings.

"Say 'gain."

"It's stupid. I was—look, never mind." A blush suffuses her cheeks.

I grasp her ass and squeeze. "Baby, you need to tell me or I'm gonna have to lick it out of you." A slick of my finger between her legs assures her I mean business. It's so hot to see and feel my come where it belongs that my dick pulses in recognition.

"You're threatening me with another orgasm?"

I thumb her clit. "You're so sensitive right now, Bean, that you'll be screaming for me to stop in seconds." I press, then rub, only to have her squirm away.

"Okay, okay! I was dancing to *'In My Feelings'* and I tripped."

"Drake's *'In My Feelings'*? Like the challenge? Did you leave your car to do that dumb dance and get run over?"

"No! I was doing it at home and I fell over the coffee table."

I roll off her and settle to her side while my body heaves with laughter.

"It's not funny! I had to Uber myself to the damn emergency room. Cat was useless. No opposable thumbs."

"Ah, baby, it's so fucking funny." I can't imagine Aubrey getting down with Drake, for a start. She's not the wildest woman I know. "Why didn't you call someone to drive you?" I would've come in a heartbeat.

"I felt like a dumbass. I was just trying to be silly. Doing something outside my usual to try to trigger a different response, I suppose."

I see how Aubrey might think that. She's lived her life following a core set of rules determined by her family. Marriage to me upended that to a certain extent, but when faced with a crisis, she fell back into familiar patterns. I wonder if we're doomed to always revert to our innate selves. Is change even possible?

"I like hearing you were trying something different. I guess that's why . . ." I stop, remembering I don't want to go there.

"Guess that's why what?"

"Why I thought I should start dating again."

Three months ago, I met someone at the bachelor party of a friend and I took her out a couple of times, once to a cookout at Max's. Aubrey was there, and it was hell to watch the betrayal on her face, one year after we'd signed the divorce papers.

"No, Grant, that was good. We had to start moving again, get ourselves out of that trench we'd dug to remain safe. I've only ever wanted you to be happy."

Which she thinks can only happen without her.

"Right back at ya, Bean."

She screws up her mouth. "I knew you'd eventually start dating and I also I knew you were going to be at Max's party. I just hadn't put both things together so quickly. So I drank a couple more glasses of wine than usual. I was pretty embarrassing."

Not that I remember. She made a few offhand comments, but she also made me smile, and damn, it had been so long since that happened. That feeling around her was enough to conclude that it was too soon for me to even think about someone new, not when I was still crazy about my ex-wife.

"You weren't. It was a defense mechanism to cope. I get that."

"And this? Us banging away while the snow falls? What's that?"

There's challenge in her voice. *Don't even think this changes a thing,* she's telling me. "Just looking to warm you up, Bean."

She laughs, and I'm filled with her light, but immediately

her smile fades. "We can't undo what happened. I've just figured out who I am without you and I need to be that person for a while."

Thing is, I don't like who I am without her, this skeletal nobody itching to care for his woman. But patience has always been rewarded when it comes to Aubrey, and I'm the most patient guy there is.

"Wouldn't dream of getting in the way of your self-improvement. And I'm definitely gonna need to see those Drake moves before the weekend's out."

CHAPTER 15

Aubrey

"Looks like we're snowed in, Bean. Storm's still raging."

I jump from the warm bed that saw plenty of action last night and pull back the drapes. White as far as I can see and still pelting against the windows like heavy, wet balls of cotton. It's Wednesday and I'd hoped to be in Boston later today in time for Thanksgiving tomorrow. "Are you sure? Couldn't we dig it out? And by 'we,' I mean you."

"It's still coming down in buckets. There's nowhere to put it and the streets are impassable. Just talked to Joanne."

"Who's Joanne?"

"Our hostess. She said they have plenty of canned soup. We'll be fine."

I peer out again, looking for a moving car or a gap in the storm that will prove Grant wrong. I see nothing to rebut his claim. Rats.

"Maybe this afternoon?"

"Weather people said it's scheduled nonstop for the next

eight hours. Maybe tomorrow. We're snowed in, wife—and you know what that means?"

I narrow my eyes, though inside my heart is in chaos at his use of "wife."

"Enlighten me."

"Sex. A lot of it. And then talking. A lot of it."

"You're the only guy I know who actually wants to talk after sex."

"And during it."

A blush heats my cheeks. Grant demonstrated some creative use of the English language last night, that's for sure. "Could we have some breakfast before this sex-and-gab fest?"

A knock sounds. Grant grins.

I throw a pillow at him. "Oh, you are so full of it, Grant Roosevelt Lincoln!"

Quickly, I scooch under the covers. Joanne—if that is her real name—needn't see all that skin. Grant goes out to the corridor, has a murmured conversation with the sainted Joanne, and comes back in with a tray. The woman has outdone herself: eggs, toast, fruit, coffee. I'm in heaven.

And looking at Grant as he starts pouring the coffee, I realize that by "heaven," what I really mean is "trouble."

"So how's Sherry doing?"

We've finished breakfast and we're snuggled under the covers. Grant's tracing circles over my left breast—it was always his favorite. Guys are weird.

"Don't want to talk about my momma right now."

Is she the "sweetheart" you were speaking to? Or maybe it was . . . "How's Zoe? She must be so tall."

He groans, and stops the careful, erotic scrutiny of my breast to grab his phone from the nightstand. A couple of taps later, and I'm scrolling through photos of last Christmas. Sherry and Jake look so happy, and as for Zoe . . . wow, she's all grown up.

"Love that girl."

"She misses you."

"I sent her gifts for the holidays and something for her birthday."

"Sweet of you." But not the same, is what he's saying. "Momma's still working at the school, keeping all the terrors in place. I think she ought to retire but I know neither Jake nor my mom would take a gift from me to move that long."

Grant's mom is a high school administrative assistant. "That's up to them, don't you think? Besides, she loves that job."

Grant frowns. He's always felt so grateful to Sherry, who had him when she was barely sixteen with no dad in the picture. It was tough for him to see Jake take over his protector role, even though he has to admit that his stepdad adores his mom.

"She's been workin' her fingers to the bone since childhood. I just want her to be happy, maybe even be a stay-at-home mom for a while."

"The woman's only forty-seven, Grant! Don't put her out to pasture just yet."

His laugh is warm and forgiving. "She always asks after you."

My heart aches. "Does she know what happened?"

"No. At first, I didn't want to worry her and then by the time we split, it seemed like it was too late to talk about it."

What have I done? I cup his jaw and trace a finger along the stubble, the sound subtle and delicious. "But you wanted to talk about it, and you kept it all in. For me."

"I know how private you are. You couldn't bear to think anyone pitied you so I handled it the way I thought would honor that."

This man. This wonderful man. But it was more than pity I feared. He fell in love with my cool, ice princess unflappability. Finding out I'm a hot mess where fissures would widen to cracks and eventually chasms would have been awful for my image.

I was mostly afraid of my husband seeing that ugly side of me.

"I shouldn't have placed that burden on you. You should have been free to confide in someone. Max, your mom, anyone." Maybe even another woman. I wonder if this will help free us both for the next stage of our lives, though the idea of Grant moving on with someone else twists my gut painfully.

A shadow crosses his face, a dark-winged bird. I've said the wrong thing. I'm always saying the wrong thing.

"Speaking of families," he says in an inelegant—for Grant—subject switch, "how are things with your dad?"

So he doesn't want to talk about us. Perhaps it's too much to expect after such a long time of not communicating. We have to work our way up to it.

"He calls when he's feeling insecure and is looking for an ego boost, especially lately in the war with my mother. He's looking for me to take a side. I need to stop caring so much."

Grant leans his chin on my shoulder. He knows my relationship with my father has always been distant. I envy Grant's family, the warmth and solidarity of it. The first time I visited Helen, Georgia, the Christmas of my second year in law school, I spent half the time in his childhood bedroom sniffling and teary-eyed.

Bean, it's Christmas. Why you wanna cry at the birth of baby Jesus?

And me, whose heart was expanding faster than my chest could withstand could only respond with, *They're all so lovely!* Followed by more sniffling. (And he still married me!) Perhaps I've underestimated his ability to handle my crazy. Perhaps bottling it up hasn't done me any favors.

"I'm not expecting much from my immediate family. This is all for my grandmother."

"At least one of them is normal—or not a complete asshole."

"You're going to behave, aren't you?"

His reaction is all mock affront. "I'm a southern gentleman, Aubrey. Good manners are in my blood and your family will only see that."

I wander my hand over his broad chest and down below the covers. "Don't need those good manners in here."

His nostrils flare. "Love a woman who knows what she wants."

I know it's just a figure of speech but that word—love—has always been so weighted between us. Grant gave it to me so easily that I couldn't possibly deserve it. After all, until I met him, no one but Libby had loved me so unconditionally.

My mother made it very clear that he had married up—and likely deliberately so. I didn't see Grant's pursuit of me in such mercenary terms. It was subtler than that, a need for Grant to fix something that was broken. The poor little rich girl was the perfect project for the gentleman protector. I was ripe for saving. And here I am, the damsel, sinking so easily into my assigned role.

I vowed I'd take back some measure of control on this trip, that I'd be the one in charge. Grant doesn't need to save me, not when I'm one of those self-rescuing princesses.

No time like the present. "I need a favor."

"Ask away."

"I want to tie you up."

"Uh . . ."

"It'll be sexy, I promise."

He considers me. "Is this all part of the plan to get your groove back?"

"It might be."

"Handcuff away."

If only I'd been that prepared! I make do with one of Grant's ties and a belt and Cat Damon gets a much-deserved vacation in the bathroom.

"Things are going to get freaky in here, kitty."

"Argghh!"

Precisely.

Grant pulls at the tie binding his right wrist to the headboard. "Now what?"

I straddle him, still in my boyshorts, but topless. "It's sweet of you to let me do this."

He rakes his gaze over my bare breasts. "Nothin' sweet about it. I expect I'm going to benefit mightily."

"Maybe, maybe not." I run a finger along the border of my underwear, then dip below.

Grant's eyes flare dangerously. "Yeah, I'm going to enjoy this."

My gaze locked onto his, I touch myself, taking long, plunging strokes through my already wet folds. He strains at the bindings, his chest heaving, his blue eyes ablaze.

For several minutes, we play this game: me stoking the fires in both of us, him watching silently. I know he could free his bonds and take over, but he doesn't. The man understands what I need right now.

Time to take it up a notch.

I grab a couple of pillows and stack them down the center, just like I did last night to separate us before we went to bed. Then I get under the comforter on the other side.

Grant groans. "Hey, I can't see."

"Exactly." I slip my panties off and resume my touch-fest, under the covers.

"Now, that's not fair, Bean."

"Sorry," I pant. "Busy getting busy." With each stroke, I

climb closer to orgasm, though it remains frustratingly out of reach.

"Talk to me," he murmurs. "Tell me how it feels."

"Wet, hot, good." My dirty talk has always been, shall we say, perfunctory.

"C'mon, baby. You can do better than that."

My eyes drift down his torso to a most satisfying tent-in-the-briefs situation. "Tell me what you'd do if your hands were free."

He takes a moment to answer. "Probably stroke my dick because it feels good and I know you love to watch."

I close my eyes, imagining that. "Then what?"

"I'd kiss those perfect tits of yours—"

"They're small."

"Perfect weight for my hands. Perfect nipples for my tongue. Perfect all round for my teeth to drag on and drive my woman wild."

I moan, not knowing if it's because of the image or the words or the desire he never fails to stir in me. My fingers rub harder, brushing my clit, prolonging the sparking sensations.

"But I wouldn't neglect that pretty pussy of yours. Oh no. I'd be comin' for that next, first with my fingers. Mine would be rougher and bigger that yours. My fingers would know exactly what you need."

My eyes flutter open, seeking out his burly body and evidence of what our game is doing to him. Every muscle is taut and his cock looks so hard it has to be hurting him.

I can't help myself. I need him to see as well as hear. Throwing back the covers and the pillow barrier, I face him on my side.

"Think my fingers are doing just fine," I tease.

He smiles, slow and sensual and so Grant. "You trying to prove you don't need a man, Bean?"

No, just that I don't need *this* man. However, I recognize that Grant watching me while I get off is probably not the self-sufficient, do-me-myself image I'm trying to cultivate. We do what we must.

The speed of my strokes picks up, the sound of friction commingling with my raspy moans. Grant never takes his eyes off me.

"That's it, baby. You're so close, I can tell. When your eyes change color—yeah, there it is."

I come hard while he talks me through it, filthy little nothings the room's soundtrack.

"My eyes change color?"

"Yeah, usually they go from gray to silver when you get emotional, but when you come, it's like sparks of blue and violet."

"You never said that before."

"Don't tell you everything, Bean. But I will tell you that watching you lettin' loose has always been the hottest thing I've ever had the pleasure to witness."

I lean in and kiss him, deeply. "What else have you never told me?"

He thinks for a moment. "Some of those sounds you make put me in mind of a possum giving birth."

I thump his arm. "Grant! I do not sound like that! And hey, I think you're forgetting that you're still tied up—"

I don't get a chance to finish that sentence because I'm flat on my back with a beautiful, beefy barrel of a man lying over me sans restraints. Hard and glorious, he slots perfectly between my thighs. I'm still sensitive and the feel of him right there where I need him is delicious.

"Guess my binding skills need work."

"Don't think you'll ever be able to keep me away." He rubs my nose, a gentle nuzzle that makes my heart swell. "No matter what happens, Bean, I'll always be here for you. Where you're concerned, I'm a lifer."

I swallow around the lump the size of a ham hock in my throat. "Quite the punishment."

"Happy to take it."

And then he proceeds to show me how happy he is.

CHAPTER 16

Grant

I just spent two hours digging out my damn car. The snowplows are on the streets so it looks like we can move. If we're lucky we'll hit Boston by Thanksgiving dinner.

I'd rather stay here. We're finally getting somewhere and dropping into the Gates fucked-up family dynamic is not going to help. But she needs to be home for her grandmother so I'll dig, dig, dig away.

Once done, I call home. "Happy Thanksgiving, Momma."

"Happy Turkey Day, hon! Aubrey's people treatin' you right?"

"We're still a few hours out. Got stuck in the Finger Lakes for a day."

"That must've been . . . interesting."

My brain downloads a moving set of images depicting the events of these last few days and what's happened between Aubrey and me. Though that makes it sound like it was truly mutual. Technically, yes. But I know in my heart of hearts that I took advantage of her. I reason that it's because Aubrey has always been so tough to crack. Any chance I have to get under her skin I have to take.

Even when she's a broken woman, still grieving her loss?

Fuck, I'm a selfish bastard. But these last few days, I've needed her just as much as she needed me.

"Grant, you still there?'

"Yeah, just thinkin'."

"Damn, I hate when you do that. When you got quiet, I knew somethin' big was going to happen. Like losing your virginity with Missy Capshaw at the lake—"

"Momma . . ."

"You powered down your vocal cords for three days while you psyched yourself up for it."

I snort. "Should I have talked it over with you first?"

"Well, it wouldn't have hurt! Could've told you that Missy wasn't worth that precious gift. Not when she already had her sights set on Tommy Jackson." No man can rightly reckon with the notion of his virginity as a precious gift, especially when expressed in the voice of his mother. "You've always been too sensitive, too caring."

Emotion clogs my throat. It's her way of saying no woman is good enough for me.

"Aubrey and her people are different from us," I reason. "She's never had that care."

"And you're the one to give it? Even at the expense of your own sanity? I just knew I'd lost you that first week of law school. When you called home and told me you'd met the woman you planned to marry."

"You never lost me, Momma. Quit bein' so dramatic."

She chuckles, owning it completely. "Grant, I just want you to be careful about that heart of yours. It's such a good one and you're such a good man."

"Only as good as the woman who raised me." That sets her off. "Momma, don't start cryin' now."

She sniffs. "If a mother can't cry to make her only son feel guilty for not being here on her favorite holiday, then what can she do?"

I laugh. "I'll be there Sunday. Three more days, Momma. Love you."

"Love you more, baby."

When I hang up, I'm left thinking on what she said. How she lost me the day I met Aubrey. I tease her about being so extra sometimes, but damn, she has the right of it.

Two days into law school, and I was still assessing the lay of the land. Who was who, who wanted to bang who, who was already banging who. Or should I say "whom."

My momma had joked that I'd come back to Helen, Georgia, talking like a Yankee, if I came back at all. (The woman sure knew how to turn those guilt screws in good and tight.) Northwestern Law on the shores of Lake Michigan in Chicago would fashion me into a regular old dandy.

But there's no changing your name, Grant Roosevelt Lincoln, she'd said—oh, only every fucking day. *You are named for three of our greatest presidents and I know you're gonna make me proud.*

No pressure, then.

This lecture hall was the largest I'd ever been in, quite a step up from Georgia Gwinnett, where I majored in business. I wasn't a complete country bumpkin. Atlanta knew how to throw a party. Hell, we had a Macy's! But Chicago had a different feel to it, for sure. Even getting coffee was weighted with significance; if you chose the wrong combination of terms for your latte, you'd betray your down-home origins.

I'd taken a seat in the Introduction to the Legal System lecture about six rows back, somewhere in the middle. While I can hold my own in a classroom, I didn't want to be lumped in with the overachievers down in front or the party kids up back. Where, and who, people gravitate to on the first day of class could tell you a lot about them.

The hall was filling up, a healthy buzz going, when a shadow entered my peripheral vision. The guy taking the seat to my right was grinning at me like a fool. Dark hair, strong features, and—there it was—a mouthful of orthodontist-perfected teeth. I'd already met him, had even heard of his family during one of my business classes at Gwinnett about the industrialization of farming in the nineteenth century.

Meet Max Henderson, meatpacking heir, trust-funder, clean-cut all-American whose last name was on a polished-gold plaque outside the lecture hall we were currently sitting in.

"Lincoln, how are you this perfect August morning?"

I sized him up. There were plenty of seats and he could have chosen to sit anywhere. We'd chatted briefly during the Taste of Northwestern Law mixer a couple of days ago, and I hated to say it—I'd liked him. I wanted to hold his wealth and looks and charm against him, but I've never been a grudge-bearer. His family name might be on the lecture hall, but he'd have to put in the work like everyone else.

"Just fine, Henderson."

He smirked, and I found myself laughing at our absurd "let's call each other by our last names" private school shtick. He opened his laptop, a top-of-the-line MacBook, and side-eyed my legal pad and pen. "Old school, huh?"

"I take better notes this way."

"You going to the game tonight?"

"Wouldn't miss it." The school had organized a bus and tickets to the Cubs game. Probably shitty seats but I was looking forward to seeing the hallowed grounds of Wrigley for the first time.

"Wanna sit in the third row behind home base?"

I snapped to attention and squinted. Hard. "Don't fuck with me, man."

He smiled. "My family has season tickets, four seats. Sure, I could be throwing back beers in the bleachers with this lot, but I figure I have three years to get to know them."

"And there are only so many Cubs games you can attend. Precious currency."

"Fuck, yeah. Cubs before the classmates I will crush with my superior brain before the year is out."

That made me laugh again. I liked his competitive streak, and while his "season tickets" thing was kind of a douche move, I wasn't going to say no.

"I'd be honored to be your plus-one at the Cubs game, Henderson."

"Losers," I heard behind me, though it sounded more like "looz-ahs."

Both Max and I turned, and that was all she wrote. Think of Snow White from the Disney cartoon. Then think of Snow White with a sheet of night-dark hair down past her shoulders, skin the color of white marble, intelligent gray eyes, and ruby-red lips I imagined would look perfect wrapped around my dick. Even with that crooked kick at the corner of her mouth that said she might give great head but your cock would get bitten off if you crossed her.

"Aubrey, your rabid Red Sox nationalism has no place here," Max said to the vision behind us. "You made your choice of law school and now you've got to live with it. Chicago all the way, baby."

My heart sank. They knew each other and it was clear as day how this was going to go down. Little details gnawed away at my self-confidence. The diamond bracelet on her slim wrist. The cut of her pale green blouse—definitely not mass-produced and definitely not green, more like chartreuse or some other fancy color terminology that trips off the tongues of women like this. And don't get me started on the name.

Aubrey.

Never had I heard a more lah-de-dah, blue blood name for a girl. Henderson had already planted a flag because green multiplies with green, and Georgia rubes raised by single mothers who worked three jobs did not win quality girls like this. Maybe if I'd mixed more at the mixer, I'd be making jokes about rabid Red Sox fans.

Max waved between us. "Lincoln, have you met . . . ?"

I was already on my feet and turning around with my arm outstretched. I wasn't about to introduce myself to this woman while sitting. My momma would've cut me with a boning knife.

"Grant Roosevelt Lincoln."

She blinked up at me, those gray eyes turning silver. Color tinged her cheeks, a watercolor blush. She swallowed, then shook her head slightly, as if to wake herself up.

"Aubrey Elizabeth Gates." She took my hand and squeezed it. Still holding on and using me as leverage, she pulled herself out of her seat. Even with the height and row differential, she was at least a foot and half shorter than me. But there was something in how she held herself, nothing small-statured about it. This woman knew how to command a room. She was used to getting what she wanted, I'd bet.

"Pleasure to meet you, Ms. Gates." I dragged on that "Ms," too.

"Southern boy?"

"Georgia to the bone."

That slight hitch to the corner of her mouth was her showing appreciation. She exuded a chilly aloofness, but that mouth was the most sensual part of her. Fires raged beneath. I intended to stoke them.

"Boston girl?" I asked, to keep the conversation going.

"My veins are filled with chowder."

Right then, my veins were filled with rocket fuel. Every cell in my body was exploding with a want I should have been questioning because this wasn't my usual. Traditionally, I had a hankering for athletic blondes, sturdy farm girls who wouldn't crumble under my rough touch. This woman had a fragility about her that terrified me, yet drew me close in rabid curiosity.

I wished she wasn't so damn tiny, though, because when I took her to bed the first time, I'd be working hard not to break her.

"Northwestern Law class of 2013," a voice called out, "welcome to Intro to the Legal System and the most grueling three years of your lives."

"You ready for this, Bean?" I asked Aubrey, this beautiful blue blood girl from Boston.

She licked her lips and my cock stirred, but damn, I didn't care if she saw it. Aubrey Elizabeth Gates should know what I was bringing.

"I'm always ready."

She released my hand and took her seat. With one last stare to record her in my brain for posterity, I turned and sat.

Out of the side of his mouth, Max muttered, "The three name strategy. Nice."

I smiled. "You trust-funders aren't the only ones with game, Henderson."

And I took that game all the way to the hoop and scored. Winning Aubrey became as important to me as graduating first in my class. I achieved both, but I hadn't reckoned on it falling apart at the first hurdle. Not a day has gone by that I don't regret not giving our marriage a little bit more room to run. Now I have a chance, and I admit I don't mind playing dirty.

I want her back.

With the car released from its snowy prison, I walk into our room at the inn to find a woman. It's Aubrey—and it's not.

The mannequin before me is perfectly put together, wearing a soft sable wool dress with a gold belt and killer heels. Her hair is smoothed back in a French knot at the nape of her neck. The clincher is the double string of pearls. After seeing her in hoodies and leggings for the last few days, I should be in awe, turned on, full of admiration.

I'm filled with dread.

Boston Aubrey is in the house—or inn. She's donned this armor to ready herself for what lies ahead.

"Thought we'd have breakfast before we check out," I say.

She picks up the cat carrier with her non-slinged arm, and I immediately take it from her with a scoot of my eyebrow.

"I'm not really hungry," she says, not looking at me. "Could we grab something from the Mickey D's drive-in? I'd like to get on the road sooner than later."

"We have another five hours to drive. Kind of fancy threads for the road."

She smooths over her skirt, as if she's just now realizing that she changed her clothes. "I don't want to have to change in a gas station restroom."

"Or maybe you need to get into a certain mindset earlier and the costume helps." I put the cat carrier on the bed, and place both of my hands on her ass, pulling her close.

"Grant," she breathes, a low, urgent sound. Never has my name sounded better on a woman's lips. I want to mess her up, inside and out.

"Aubrey, these last couple of days have been—"

"Wonderful," she finishes, "but probably more because we've both been feeling blue and lonely."

I can't deny that, but she makes it sound like it was purely a function of proximity and depression. "So any hot mouth and clever fingers would do?"

She narrows her eyes. "Are you going to make a big thing out of this? I can't deal with it, Grant. Not today."

Not when she needs to psyche herself up for a visit to the Lion's Den. Or the Lioness's—Marie-Claire Gates. Aubrey has a largely dysfunctional relationship with her mother, a woman who demands perfection from everyone around her. I refused to play Momma Gates's games, so we didn't gel, though I tried for Aubrey's sake. Maybe I could have tried harder.

Today I will, if only to support my ex-wife as we prepare to descend on the Thanksgiving from hell.

~

FIVE HOURS later we're winding through the narrow streets of Back Bay—Boston drivers are the worst—as the air in the stuffily-hot car chills by the second. Out of the corner of my eye I can see Aubrey wringing her hands while her shallow breaths are our soundtrack.

I pull the car over and put on the hazards. Some Red Sox–loving Masshole behind me slams on the horn then overtakes me with a few choice words. I've heard worse in court.

"It's around the corner," she says.

"Uh-huh. We need to talk about how it's going to go down."

"Go down?"

"I know I'm here so we can break the news gently to your grandmother, but maybe we don't have to."

"What?"

I need to be careful. "Maybe we tell everyone that we've reconciled. Takes the pressure off, so we don't need to present one face to your family and another to Libby. You can act a little easier around them, not worry so much about what everyone's thinking and just focus on enjoying the holiday."

She's looking at me like I'm mad. Maybe I am.

"Aubrey? Got any comment?"

"But we haven't reconciled," she says in a tone of *and it ain't never gonna happen.* "I can probably fake it for an hour or two with Libby, but the entire time?"

I lean in and grasp both her hands, warming them in mine. Her body visibly relaxes at my touch. "You won't have to fake it. Not after we've cleared the air. We're healing, Bean."

Her eyes widen, tears imminent. There was a time I couldn't bear them but now I welcome anything that spells release for Aubrey.

"We are, aren't we?" she whispers.

I nod.

"But that doesn't mean we're fixed." Sounds like she's trying to convince herself. "Eventually I have to tell Libby that we're divorced."

Not if I have anything to do with it. "Let's play it by ear. This way people won't be tiptoeing around us *and* your grandmother. We can relax."

She scrunches up her pretty red mouth. "It's not your worst idea."

"That's my girl." I release her and put the car in drive again. "Let's do this."

CHAPTER 17

Aubrey

We park around the back in one of the garages, which also means we can sneak through the kitchen and not make a big to-do about our arrival.

"Someone can get that," I say, referring to the luggage Grant is unloading from the trunk.

He raises an eyebrow.

"Okay, carry it yourself, peasant."

Provoked, he drops the bags and stalks over to me.

"What are you doing?"

"I think maybe you need to relax a little."

I know what Grant's idea of relaxing involves and it's probably going to scandalize the neighbors. Also, I'm still reeling from his plan amendment a few moments ago. *You won't have to fake it. We're healing, Bean.*

Likely, he doesn't intend it this way, but it's almost cruel. I'm feeling far too hopeful, which means it's about to turn to shit. I don't know if we're healing; I do know that I'm relying on Grant far too much to get there.

"Don't you dare—"

He lifts me off the ground and kisses me hard. I can't help it—I melt into him. Every moment with him since we left Chicago has been the cut and the salve. Even with the pain, I feel as though it's bearable, possibly worth it just to feel something again. Anything. His tongue slips inside my mouth, tangles with mine, and sets off sparks through every nerve ending in my body. He cups my ass, and it's perfect. I'm practically climbing him like a tree, eager to get closer, inside him.

Slowly he draws back, his eyes glassy and unfocused. Pride mixed with power warms my chest.

"Okay, I'm relaxed," I say with a husky chuckle.

He pushes his erection against my stomach. "But now I'm not."

"Guess you shouldn't have started it, then?"

"Worth it."

Another voice intrudes. "Aubrey, what on earth are you doing?"

"There goes my hard-on," Grant mutters, to which I laugh because, damn, I've missed him and how he's always been able to cut through my prickliness. No one has ever nurtured me like Grant. Yet again, I wonder what he's getting out of the deal.

I turn, knowing that my lipstick is probably smeared and nowhere near the perfection my mother expects. I could say I don't care but it'd be a lie. I do. I always have. Marie-Claire Amiens Gates stands before me, the model of French chic and disapproval.

"Hi, Mom," I say, feeling shy.

Her lips thin because I haven't called her "Maman." That's what she encouraged—no, insisted—my brothers and I call her as children. She doesn't want "Maman" because of some long-standing family tradition, but because it set us apart from other families. American riffraff, as she called them, despite the fact they were often just as wealthy as the Gates.

The Gates don't exactly go back to the *Mayflower*. Think more along the lines of the Astors or the Vanderbilts, that kind of rich. We have homes in Boston, the Cape, St. Bart's, London, and Paris. Our multinational company rivals Berkshire Hathaway for capitalization.

Both of my brothers work for the company, VPs of something invented to justify their large salaries and epic trust funds. They're not bad people, just entitled.

You're going to law school, Aubs? Bradford said when he heard. *But . . . why? You've got a job right here!*

I know I'm not like them. Yet I still crave my mother's approval because I'm a mass of contradictions and a scared little girl. Now I blink at her, conscious that my ex-husband still has his hands on my ass and doesn't seem inclined to let go.

"Mom, skulking about in the garage? That doesn't seem your style."

She shrugs. "I was at the club seeing about some last-minute party planning for your grandmother and had just parked next door when I heard you come in." Her gaze moves past me. "Grant, *comment ca va?*"

"*Ca va bien,* Marie-Claire," Grant replies in perfect French, surprising me, but not my mother. She'd never be so gauche as to display true shock, but she'd be cruel enough to try to embarrass an outsider by speaking in a foreign language.

"Well, everyone is looking forward to seeing you," she says, looking me up and down. "Come into the salon when you have freshened up."

That I don't pass muster, though I paid special attention to my clothes, hair, and makeup, doesn't go unnoticed. She doesn't ask about my arm in a sling. Neither does she close the gap to hug me even though we haven't seen each other in two years.

We're not the most demonstrative of families. Any wonder I'm a coldhearted, prickly-skinned bitch? Not that Grant has ever called me that. I know what I am. I know what I distill to when my confidence wanes.

"Mom," I say, feeling emboldened. "Something's changed. Grant and I—"

"Grant and you?" she cuts in.

"We've reconciled. We're together again."

My mother's face remains as impassive as the granite statues lining the main drive to the house. "We'll talk about it later."

With one last once-over, my mother leaves, and I let out the breath I've been holding.

"That went . . . okay?" I say, squinting at Grant.

"Could've been worse. She could've commented on my massive erection."

~

MY GRANDMOTHER, Elizabeth Amelia March Gates—who's better known as, and insists she be called, Libby—lives in what we call the Dower Tower, a sumptuous wing of the family's Back Bay mansion. Not a tower at all, it sports a castle turret as its most prominent feature and it's where she moved when my grandfather died twenty-eight years ago, thus vacating the primary estate for her son and his wife in true feudal fashion.

Libby has lived her life refusing to be circumscribed by age, gender, or assholes. She tried her hand as a director in Hollywood in the forties (*Acting's for morons,* she likes to say. *I mean, children can do it*), flew crop dusters in the fifties (*All the good pilots were in Korea, someone had to step up*), had a brief stint as a *Playboy* bunny in the sixties (*Hefner was a terrible lay, Elvis was as scrumptious as he looked*), and became the first female CEO of a stock-exchange-listed company.

She scares the shit out of me and I love her with total abandon.

"Aubrey!"

As I walk in, Grant takes my hand. Why is he being so perfect, especially when I don't deserve his kindness? A brief urge to blurt out the truth crawls up my throat. *It's all fake, Libby. I'm the biggest phony there is.*

Grant's holding Cat Damon in his other arm. They've been getting along well these last few days, which makes me think the cat shrink knows of what she speaks. Neither has the cat tried to chew any of my bras.

But I forgot about Asta—that's Libby's fox terrier. On spying my cat, he starts barking.

Cat Damon jumps down, hisses a cheery greeting, and stands his ground.

A chastened Asta slinks away behind the sofa.

Good talk.

I let go of Grant's hand and bend over my grandmother. She's in a wheelchair, looking frailer than I've ever seen her. Her hair is dyed-to-the-roots strawberry blond—it's her one vanity—and she's pulled it back in a chignon. Her skin feels paper-thin as I land a kiss on her cheek.

"You've lost weight," Libby says, her rheumy eyes assessing me. "And you look tired. Not the good kind, either." She shoots an accusatory glance at Grant that proclaims him negligent in his husbandly duties. I could tell her that the man has more than compensated for the neglect in the last couple of days, but she has a filthy mind and would insist on details.

"I'm fine," I say quickly. "Oh, Libby, it's so good to see you. I'm sorry it's been so long."

My grandmother scoffs. "Why should you young people make time for us ancients? Never apologize for living your life." She turns to her assistant, a guy who looks like the product of an inadvisable Mr. Clean and The Rock union. "Make yourself useful, Jordie. Double gin fizz."

"You know what the doctor said." So little conviction exists in Jordie's tone that I suspect this is an exchange they have regularly to keep things interesting.

"I made it this far on a gin fizz a day. Worried a double will make me live longer? You're not in the will!"

I laugh, loving her irreverence, before adding, "Grant's here."

"So I see, strapping as ever. If I could do it over, I'd pick a bull of a man like you did." Before I can protest this objectification—and frankly, what would be the use?—she reaches out her hand to Grant. "Come here, hot stuff, let me get a better look at you. My eyes aren't what they once were."

Grant's smile is genuine, which makes me so happy, and he leans in to kiss my grandmother on the cheek. "Still rabble-rousing, sweetheart?"

"The rabble could do with some rousing, don't you think? Especially this lot. It's like the Cold War with your parents, Aubrey. Neither of them will give in and move out. It's just a house!" She shoos us toward the sofa. "Now tell me what you two have been up to."

Over my gin fizz, I spend the next hour lying through my teeth.

Everything is fine. My job is amazing. Chicago is the best place on earth, even with the horrid winters. We drove around Spain this summer and even spent a week in Iceland. After a while I start to believe we're the super couple we've always been.

My phone buzzes with a message from my mother. *Join me for tea in the little salon.* Because we have two.

"Summoned by the lady of the manor?" my grandmother says. She's not a fan of her current daughter-in-law, with whom my father cheated while he was still married to the first Mrs. Gates, a woman who's been relegated to history and a mansion in Miami Beach. Neither is she a fan of her son or even her grandsons, my half-brothers. That I've left her for so long in this "nest of vipers," as she calls them, eats away at me.

"Dinner with the lot of them will be in ninety minutes," she says, "so I'll see you for cocktails in an hour."

"Triple gin fizzes all around." I stand, smoothing my skirt nervously. My gaze falls on the Christmas tree, trimmed perfectly with ornaments inscribed with the names of family members, past and present. It's a strange tradition for someone with as much sentimentality as a tree trunk. She stole it from the soap opera *Days of Our Lives*.

"Tree's up early this year." I touch one of the ornaments, a green one with Grant's name on it sitting next to a red one with mine. My heart clenches.

"Jordie wanted to get it over with," she says, though I don't believe her.

"Need me to come with you?" Grant asks as I make a move to the door.

"He can stay with me," Libby says.

I eye my grandmother carefully. "As long as you're not too tired."

"Not too tired to say all the filthy things to your husband that I've been holding back."

"Libby!" I giggle, a lightness lifting me because the two people in my corner are right here. Then I remember who I need to talk to next, and that cloud follows me out of the Dower Tower.

I enter the little salon to find my mother is already pouring tea, its aromatic scent familiar and comforting. She slides an unsubtle glance at her Cartier watch because I'm late for a meeting that has no official start time.

"Entrez, chérie," she says, though I'm already inside. It's said to retroactively give me permission.

I'm not feeling my usual subservient self today, probably because chatting with Libby and the support from Grant has put me in a good mood. I'm determined to hold on to it and the good vibes of the last couple of days.

She puts a sugar cube in my tea even though I take neither tea or sugar. When she hands the cup and saucer to me, I place it down on the coffee table.

"Is Dad here?" I ask. He lives on one side of the house, as both refuse to leave, despite the fact they could afford any number of sumptuous townhouses. It's the principle of the thing.

"He's at the office."

"On Thanksgiving?"

"Gates is a global firm, Aubrey. The markets don't close in other countries." She sips her tea. "I don't understand why Grant is here."

"We've been seeing each other lately," I lie, "and he wanted to come with me for Libby's birthday party."

"But I thought it was all behind you. That you'd come to realize how incompatible you are."

"You're the only one who thought that, Mom."

"Yet you divorced him." The words are heavy with my failure. I suppose I should have remained locked in thirty years of misery like my parents. "You had to have a reason."

She's right—and that's a rare conclusion to draw about something my mother says. I know my miscarriage set us on that road but it didn't have to end in divorce court. Plenty of couples overcome their grief. Instead, we fell apart. And a couple of days jumping each other's bones shouldn't make it hunky-dory again.

"There are always reasons." I pick up a shortbread cookie and take a bite. At my mother's faint lip twitch of disapproval, I stuff the whole thing in my mouth.

Her expression proclaims me childish. "Well, I know he didn't cheat on you."

"How do you know that?"

She makes a very French noise of discontent that pronounces her an expert on such matters. Having been on both sides of it, I've no doubt she is.

"How he looks at you, then and now, it's . . . obsessive. No man should be that crazy about his wife. It's not healthy and it inevitably leads to disappointment. A man like Grant has appetites, cravings, and if you can't satisfy them . . ." She waves a hand to finish.

"If I can't satisfy them, what?"

"If you're unable to give him what he needs, then this is your fault. It's always the woman's fault."

"Are you saying that's how society—or your concept of society—views it or are you saying it actually is the woman's fault if she can't somehow hold on to her man?"

She arches an eyebrow at my lawyerly deconstruction of her statement. My ability to parse an argument is why I'm excellent at what I do and not nearly as successful in my personal life. I have a tendency toward overanalysis and second-guessing.

"Men are fickle—"

"Except when they're unhealthily obsessed with their wives."

She sighs as if I could never understand. "Grant's background has always been too different from yours. No father. A teen mother bringing him up. All that . . . working-class struggle."

She's such a snob. "What about my background? A

neglectful father. A mother more concerned with turning me into a society debutante so I could marry well."

"I wanted nothing but success for you."

The implication being that she could have destroyed me based on my suspect origins but chose not to. I often wonder what possessed her to take on the child of her husband's indiscretion. Surely, it should have been the last straw yet she elected instead to mold me into a creation she could be proud of. Unfortunately, every day I disappoint her.

She truly believes she did the best she could and calling her out at this point won't change a thing. We're the equivalent of cable news talking heads shouting at each other from opposing ends of the spectrum.

I resolve to change the topic. "How's the party planning going?"

"*Comme ci, comme ça*. I didn't expect you to have a guest. As I said, Mason Van Giet will be there and I told him you were available."

"Sorry to upend your matchmaking plans."

My mother cocks her head, takes a good hard look at me. "I don't believe you're back together for a second. It's all a little too convenient."

I could never get anything past her, yet today I'm determined to try.

"We're healing, Mom. Slowly, but we're getting there. So how about you stop treating him like the help and start giving him the respect the man I chose deserves?"

She raises an eyebrow. "A little late for that."

Maybe she's right. Maybe it's a little late for everything.

CHAPTER 18

Grant

With Aubrey gone, I brace myself for some real talk from Libby, but first she commands me to wheel her to the greenhouse. It takes up about eight hundred square feet on the south side of the apartment, though "apartment" is a very loose description for where Libby lives.

The greenhouse has a Victorian-era feel to it, and entering it is like stepping back in time. My mother gardens so I recognize some plants, mostly hothouse flowers that really don't belong in this part of the country. But humans can't help forcing things into environments where they shouldn't. I obey her instructions to push her chair down one aisle, stopping on command so she can finger ferns and pat soils.

"Wait—is that a cannabis plant?" We've come to the end of one row, and tucked away at the back is . . . shit, a whole garden of herbals.

"It's legal."

"Six plants are legal in the Commonwealth of Massachusetts, Libby. This is an enterprise."

"I need it for my arthritis. Do you know how hard it is to get a dealer to the house?"

Jesus. I so don't need to hear this.

"Why is my granddaughter still lying to me?"

I grimace. "Did you think I could just turn it around in a couple of days and undo years of what this family has inflicted on her?"

"I suppose it was too much to hope that your magic penis would produce the results I want."

I feel my color rising. Aubrey is more like her grandmother than anyone, and I wish she could take that fuck-you attitude and ride it all the way through her life. "She's *your* granddaughter. Nothing is easy."

She barks out a joyless laugh. "All this time I've been waiting for her to confide in me, to share with me her pain."

I say quietly, "I've been waiting, too."

Libby and I gelled from the start, and for the last year and a half, we've been phone buddies. FaceTime, actually, because she does better when we have the visuals. About six months after I separated from my wife, Libby called me, because she knew something was terribly wrong.

I broke down on the phone and told her everything. Christ, I haven't even told my mother, and there I was sobbing like a schoolkid to the equivalent of Katherine Hepburn.

I thought that sharing might help Aubrey, but I begged Libby to wait until Aubrey reached out herself. If my ex-wife knew I'd told someone in her family about the baby . . . shit, she'd never speak to me again. My moment of weakness, my need to grieve my lost child to someone who would understand had overcome me. But Aubrey still hasn't told another living soul. I wonder if she ever will or if she's pushed it down so deep that she's convinced herself it need never find voice.

If I'm the only person she wants to talk to about this, then I can be there for her. I can be the sponge that absorbs all her pain. But I think it would be better for her mental health if she let her grandmother in. She doesn't get a lot of affection in this family, but her relationship with her grandmother has always been a shining light. The old dame's a sharp one, but she has a soft side, too. Just like Aubrey.

"She can't know I told you. I'm hoping—praying that she'll unburden with you this weekend. Just give her time."

"I know how to handle my granddaughter, Grant."

I roll my eyes. "It's not a fucking contest, Lib."

She hates when I call her that, but she likes that I stand up to her.

Jordie pops his head around the door to the greenhouse and calls out. "Tea, Mrs. G?"

"No, I'm ready to dress for dinner."

I am dismissed.

By the time I make it over to the other wing of the house, I can tell the energy in the house is different. I should probably change into formal evening wear, but Aubrey might need me and I'm pretty whipped when it comes to that girl.

I head to the lounge. People congregate here before dinner and that's where I find most of the Gates, including Aubrey's oldest brother, her sister-in-law, their kids, and assorted aunts, uncles, and cousins. The room looks like an episode of *Downton Abbey* with heavy oil paintings of ancestors, an ornate fireplace, and fussy furniture that might fall apart if you sat on it. (Or if *I* sat on it.)

And then I see her.

Aubrey's on a red velvet sofa, holding a baby. From my regular check-ins with the family's matriarch, I gather this is Aubrey's newest niece, who's about eight months old. No one has seen me yet so I watch from the doorway, gauging her reaction. Seeing that baby in the diner the day before yesterday unlocked something in her—and I'm still not sure if it's positive or negative. Aubrey's own flesh and blood is a different thing, however.

The baby sits in her lap and Aubrey is nuzzling their noses together. The child is loving it, gurgling and laughing, reacting like any child would. And Aubrey? She's holding her own.

She turns to me, and that smile of hers crashes through me, bright and so, so sharp. Sunshine blooms and burns in my chest.

"Grant!" The piercing sound is Janice, my ex-sister-in-law, who I'm pretending is my current sister-in-law. She's sweet as peach tea but kind of scattered.

She grasps my arm, a quick, harried breath blowing blond curls out of green eyes. "God, you look good! Really, really good! I thought you and Aubs were caput!"

I open my mouth, but she's still talking, every few words punctuated by exclamation points.

"Well, I always thought you were perfect together but Tristan said—" She cuts off and covers her mouth. "Sorry, I didn't mean that!"

"It's okay, Janice. I know what Tristan thinks." Neither of Aubrey's brothers likes me and while I'd appreciate that sentiment if it came from a place of protectiveness for their sister, I know that's not it. They think I'm gold-digging white trash.

I smile to put her at ease. "How've you been?"

"Oh, good. The kids are torture." Reminded she's a parent, she grabs the shoulders of one of them, Thatcher, a towheaded gangster who must be close to ten. A Twizzler hangs out of the side of his mouth like a cigarette. "I told you to stop eating candy, Thatch! We're having dinner any minute! Say hi to your uncle Grant who came all the way from Chicago to see you!"

Thatcher and I exchange appropriately skeptical glances. "Uh, hi." He turns to his mother. "I thought Aunt Aubrey dumped him because he's a redneck."

"What? No! I never said that. No one ever said that!" Janice blushes as red as Aubrey's dress. "I said—oh, never mind. Go find your sister and wash your hands before dinner. Sheesh!"

Thatcher bounds off, leaving Janice with her mouth gaping, floundering in the rubble of an episode of *Kids Say the Darndest Things*.

"I've no idea how he comes up with this stuff."

"Out of the mouths of babes," I say to smooth over her gaffe. I really don't care.

"Babes?" Janice giggles and leans in. "That's *so* sweet of you. I don't get a lot of compliments these days. But, uh, married woman, you horndog!" She holds up her ring finger dramatically.

I could explain I wasn't coming on to her but what would be the point? Like I said, sweet but scattered.

Inane small talk has never been my style but Janice has a habit of covering both sides of the conversation. I'm happy to let her because it gives me a chance to check out Aubrey. The peace doesn't last, however.

"Lincoln!"

Aubrey's oldest brother invades my personal space. Both bros are back-slapping, Masters of the Universe assholes, but this one wins by a hair.

They have names—Tristan and Bradford—but I prefer to think of them as Dumb and Dumber. Not that they're all that stupid, but they think I am because I'm from the South, and nothing gets my goat more than Northerners making assumptions because of how I talk. Aubrey isn't close to them, so it's never been a source of conflict for us, yet their neglect of her bothers me because it's a symptom of everything that is wrong with this family.

Tristan is in his mid-thirties and does something with marketing at Gates Inc., though you wouldn't know it because the guy can't promote himself out of a paper bag.

"Thought you and Aubs packed it in, sport?"

"Didn't stick. Giving it another go."

"Maman's not going to like that. She already has someone lined up for her."

My muscles tense at the notion Aubrey's being prepared like a lamb on the altar of the Boston marriage mart. Not on my watch.

"No worries, *sport*. Aubrey and I just need a little space to ourselves to work this out."

"Well, it'll be good for Libby, I suppose." He eyes me suspiciously. "Of course, she probably won't last long, so if you're just faking it for her, it wouldn't be terrible for her to find out. Might move things along, you know?"

"Tristan!" Janice is horrified. "Must you say everything that pops into your head?"

"You mean, like you?"

"Gonna go talk to my girl," I say, moving off.

"Pussy-whipped," Tristan observes wisely as he gulps down another mouthful of scotch.

I walk over, ignoring the hellos from other family members, all inflected with "fancy seeing you here." My goal is my wife. It always has been.

Taking a seat, I ask, "So who's this?"

"Grant, meet Minerva."

"Oh, poor Minerva," I mutter in commiseration.

"Stop," Aubrey whispers with a giggle. "It's lovely. I'm calling her Minnie but Janice says I shouldn't." She pulls a face. "I'm sorry. I should have mentioned that Tristan and Janice had another child."

As I can't tell her I already knew from my regular chats with her grandmother, I shrug it off. "Life goes on, Bean."

Her smile is genuine and genuinely lovely. "Yes, it does, doesn't it?"

We lock gazes for a long moment, another check in the healing.

"How's your mom?"

She sighs. "The same. It's impossible to tell if she wants me here or would rather never see me again. I'd like to think I fulfill *some* function for her."

Marie-Claire's affection has always been transactional, so the function idea isn't far off. My heart keens for Aubrey. Her family life is so the opposite of mine, which factors into our very different communication styles. I wish we were in Georgia, where Aubrey could live and breathe a blueprint for family love and laughter.

Aubrey coughs slightly. "How were things with Libby?"

"Peachy. She's always adored me." Aware that I need to encourage Aubrey to open up to her family before Libby forces the issue, I start laying the groundwork. "She's worried about you. Can tell you're a bit down."

"No Oscars for me this year."

"She wants to be there for you."

"I don't need to worry her now. Not when—not when we've figured out a way to get through this so she won't get hurt."

"Continue to lie?"

She blanches and lowers her voice. "This was your idea."

Sure, but I expected it wouldn't be long before we couldn't tell the difference. Hell, I can't, which means I'm in serious fucking trouble here.

A change of tack is needed. "So you and I work with some

pretty hurt people, clients who are going through amazingly stressful situations. Have any of them ever broken down in front of you?"

"Of course."

"You ever notice when that happens that they seem to let go of the grudges they've been holding on to? That the case suddenly becomes easier for everyone involved?"

"So they get a release. There's lots of ways to do that. More enjoyable ways than bleeding out every single emotion, Grant."

She means sex. If Aubrey thinks that the release she gets from orgasms is going to solve all her problems, then she's in for a rude awakening. I mean, I'm good but . . .

"Maybe you ought to try it. Lose your shit with your mom, tell your dad he's an ass, come clean with your grandmother. Might be liberating, Bean."

She turns to Minnie and rocks her on her knee. "What do you think, Minnie? Should I throw a tantrum like a big baby? Will that get me everything I've ever wanted?"

Minnie offers up a watery giggle in response.

"Sounds like Minnie agrees with me," I say.

Aubrey remains silent. So she's not ready to fight back yet, but before this weekend is through I'm going to have her boxing like a heavyweight champ.

"So where's Brad?" I haven't seen any sign of her other brother, the Dumber in the equation.

"In Bora Bora with his girlfriend." She shrugs, unsurprised, but I can tell she's hurt. "He won't make it back for Libby's party."

The disappointments, they keep on coming. However, just when I think her family has no more bullshit to offer, they pull another rabbit out of their hats.

"Aubrey, my girl!"

The master of the house has arrived.

CHAPTER 19

Aubrey

My father is a good-looking man, perpetually well groomed and turned out, who thinks he's much more charming than he truly is. His weakness is women, except when it comes to his only daughter. I've never been a daddy's girl. I'm a reminder of his mistake, and while I'm just one of many, I'm the only one that followed him home.

Since he and my mother announced their thirty-years-in-the-making split, he's become more attentive to me, a ploy to ensure I'll remain on the right side of the newly drawn battle lines. Inspiring loyalty was never his strong suit, but these days he's conscious of his age and has become strangely maudlin.

Holding the baby is the perfect excuse not to have to hug him, but Janice whips Minnie out of my hands, leaving me ready and able to greet my father.

"Hi, Dad. Happy Thanksgiving."

"Honey, you look tired." He cups my chin and examines

my face. Sometimes I wonder if he's looking for the ghost of the woman who gave me life. We never talk about her. "What happened to your arm?"

"Oh, just something silly. The worst is I can't drive."

"Still terrified of planes?" His chuckle isn't malevolent, just puzzlement that one of his children could show such a strange weakness.

"Still terrified of wrinkles, Jeffrey?" My mother's sniping contribution. Though it's framed as a defense of me, I know it's not meant as one. Just another chance to score points.

Still, the wrinkles comment has me checking my father's unusually smooth forehead, which must be Botoxed. He's the vainest person I know.

"Lincoln!" My father grabs Grant's hand and pumps it. "Didn't expect to see you here. I thought—"

"We've reconciled, Dad," I cut in, "and we're keeping our former situation on the down low for Libby, okay? As far as she knows, we've been fine forever."

"Got it," he says blithely because he's not really paying attention. He looks over his shoulder, oddly agitated. "I want you to meet someone. Mercedes, come say hello to my daughter."

A redhead in a shimmery blue cocktail dress has just entered the room; she must have been waiting outside until summoned. She's at least ten years younger than me.

"You've brought a guest to Thanksgiving dinner," my mother says, sounding both bored and furious.

"Hello!" The new arrival—Dad's current girlfriend, I gather—is as edgy as a high-strung Thoroughbred. I'm torn between pity for her, sympathy for my mother, and rage at my father for being even more of a dick than usual. "I'm Mercedes. Like the car."

I open my mouth to put her at ease, but distracted by Grant, she blinks up at him like a child seeing Santa for the first time. "God, you're a big 'un!" She won't stop looking at him. I completely understand, but still, I can't have that.

"Hi, Mercedes. I'm Aubrey."

"Oh, hi, I heard *all* about you from Jeff." As if realizing that doesn't sound as nice as it could, she adds quietly. "You're so lovely."

My ex-husband offers with a half grin, "I've always thought so."

A warm gooey feeling wars with the acid in my stomach. No one knows quite what to do with the situation, except Grant, who isn't burdened with the baggage of the rest of us.

"Mercedes, I'm guessing you're not from around here. I'm hearing New York? Maybe Queens?"

"Oh, you're good!" Mercedes looks immensely relieved. "You think New Yorkers are unfriendly? Nothing like Boston!" Color flushes her cheeks. "Oh, I didn't mean—"

"It's okay," I say. "Bostonians can be tough nuts to crack."

"Yeah, they take assholery to peak levels," Grant comments dryly, which sends Mercedes into a hoot of nervous laughter.

While they launch into a spirited conversation on all the reasons Boston and its denizens suck, I pull my father aside. "Dad, I know you're trying to make Mom's life a living hell, but this is such a crazy dick move."

My father takes a slug of scotch. "Just looking to encourage that French witch out the door."

I close my eyes. *Why I'm a basket case? Exhibit A, Your Honor.*

"So how's my girl? Made partner yet?"

"Not quite. But I'm the managing associate of the family law division and I had an article published in the *Journal of . . .*"

My father's not paying attention, too busy checking in on my mother's reaction. She's playing with Minnie and chatting with my awesome sister-in-law, Janice, doing a fine job of not buying in to his bullshit.

"Yeah, that's great, sweetheart. How's your grandmother?"

You mean, your *mother, Dad? How's* your *mother?*

"She'll have plenty to say about your visitor."

He hums his agreement. "She can't stand Marie-Claire either so we're probably all good there."

Give. Me. Strength.

I glance over my father's shoulder to see how Grant is doing. Of all the people in this room, I like him and Minnie the best. His solidity never fails to ground me, ballast in the storm. Maybe I'm just reaching for a life preserver during these shit show days with the fam. Maybe what I'm feeling isn't real. For so long, I've doubted my instincts.

Grant is letting Mercedes talk, nodding at whatever she's saying. He catches my eye and winks, and I'm assured that maybe I'm not the craziest person in the room after all.

After more than two hours of torture later—the passive-aggressive sniping at the dinner table was legendary—I knock on my mother's door and wait. It takes about thirty seconds, during which I imagine she's fixing her makeup and donning a peignoir. When the door opens, I'm surprised to see her in a Red Sox T-shirt, yoga pants, and thick socks. She looks positively human.

"I know it's late but I wondered if we could talk."

"Of course. Come in, *chérie.*"

As a child, my mother's room was off-limits, her sanctuary from the household she was raising without my father. Oh, he was there on the boundaries but he had an empire to run. My brothers' cynical take was that Marie-Claire knew what she was getting herself into when she broke up the first marriage of a man like Jeffrey Gates. Two stepsons and a daughter she was forced to adopt were her penance.

On the TV, people are speaking French with no English

subtitles. She mutes it and takes a seat on a love seat near the window, patting the cushion beside her.

"Is this about Grant?"

"No, this isn't about Grant. Tell me what's going on with Dad."

Two spots of color appear high on her cheeks. "He's going through one of his phases. It'll pass."

"You're in the middle of a divorce and neither of you want to budge. But you're okay with him bringing his girlfriend to Thanksgiving dinner. Some phase." She should have gone ballistic but that's just not done in Casa Gates.

"Aubrey, you don't understand."

"Help me understand, then. Help me figure out why you" —*let him steamroll you into raising me as your own*—"don't just take the settlement and run." I've no doubt it's a good deal, a nice lump sum that will keep her in luxury for the rest of her life.

"He owes me. For what I had to put up with. The affairs, all of it."

The *result* of his affairs, that's what she means. I don't know why I bother.

"It's not like you can get more than half. Even a quarter is a fortune. You'll never want for anything again."

"Maybe I want more than money."

I close my eyes, amazed at the human capacity for self-delusion. "You want him back. After everything he's done, you would take him back."

"I know he wasn't the most attentive father but he had work to do supporting us all with the company. You never wanted for a thing."

"That's not the problem—"

"You had horse-riding lessons, ballet, parties the envy of every girl on the East Coast. And that's all because your father spoiled you rotten."

"I'm not saying none of that is true, but this isn't about me. Why are you defending him? He's always been selfish and distant, with an ego as big as all outdoors. I don't even remember you sharing a room."

"So you're an expert on marriage now, Aubrey? The girl who chose rashly and now can't make up her mind about whether her husband is ex or not."

I don't understand it. I've *never* understood their relationship. I always thought it was because I was too young to interpret the nuances but I should get it by now. I could say the heart wants what it wants but that assumes Marie-Claire has a working cardiac muscle. Does my mother hold on out of spite? Whatever it is, clearly she has no intention in confiding in me.

"I'm not claiming to be an expert. Grant and I have had our problems but we're working them out. He's here because he cares about me. Even at our lowest, he never treated me like Dad treated you tonight."

But he did start dating. He brought that woman to Max's party a few months ago. He tried to move on because he . . . was *ready* to move on. The conclusion pokes me with the force of a sharp stick.

Grant's not here for himself and he's certainly not here to win me back. He's on site to help me move on. My chest warms at the care in that gesture, then chills at the true meaning of it.

This is a slow burn to the end.

"You and I have never been close, so I'm not expecting a miracle now," I offer, "but if you need my help for anything, I'm here."

Her eyes widen, and for a brief second, I wonder if she might squeeze out a tear. "I've only ever wanted the best for you, Aubrey, so you would never have to worry about whether a man loved you or not. So it wouldn't be so important."

Toughening me up in the name of ensuring my happy man-free independence? Is that a fucking French thing?

"But love is important, Mom. Unselfish, unconditional love." The kind that Grant is giving me now, a generosity of spirit I can never hope to emulate. "In fact, it might be the most important thing of all."

CHAPTER 20

Grant

As if Max knows I'm alone, with enemies at the gates, he chooses the moment Aubrey goes to talk to her mother to call me.

"Hey, happy Turkey Day, Lincoln."

Still with the last name shtick. He doesn't realize it but he got me through these last couple of years.

"You at your parents?"

"Yeah, full-on with all the Hendersons after lunch with Charlie's folks. Thought I'd better call before it gets too late. How's it going?"

"Well, I'm still alive. And so's the cat."

"And Aubrey?"

"Things are in flux but we're talking, which is a start."

A lengthy pause ensues while his brain churns. Finally, he says, "You know I never pried because I was in the mindset of 'of course it failed—that's what happens.'"

"Except for your parents, the model for marital perfection."

"Hell, the two of them are freaks." He sighs. "What I'm trying to say is that I assumed the reasons behind the failure of my best friends' marriage were incredibly private and none of my damn business. But sometimes I'd see you hurting and I didn't push when I think maybe I should have. Maybe I should have been a nosey fucker after all."

I pinch the bridge of my nose, wishing away the headache that's developed behind there.

"Are you saying you'd like to know now, Max?"

"Only if you want to share. But if you and Aubs are on the road to somewhere good and you'd rather I just butt out, say that, too."

Aubrey could be back any minute and who knows if this needs to come out now. But I'm tired of holding it in, how taut my muscles feel all the time, how sensitive my feet feel dancing over those eggshells. I head into the en suite bathroom, shut the door, and sit on the toilet. The cat scratches at the door, so I let him in.

"M&*#%!"

Settling him into my lap, I close my eyes, dreading the shape of the words. "We lost a baby, Max. A miscarriage."

Silence for a long beat, then, "Fuck."

Yeah. Fuck.

I begin the process of laying my internal organs bare to my closest friend, the memory as sharp now as the day it happened.

I'd just come home from work and needed to change for dinner with Max and this girl he was dating. As Max rarely took a woman out a second time, I suspected this would be an incredible waste of everyone's time.

I let out a low whistle.

"What?" Aubrey waved a hand from neck to hip, taking in a ruby red dress she knew I adored for the wondrous silhouette it gave to her body. "This old thing."

"Don't want to go," I muttered. "Don't want to see stupid Max, who I work with and just saw an hour ago, hamming it up with some girl he's going to bang once and never see again." In a mini-tantrum, I ripped off my tie and threw it on the floor. My shirt was next.

Aubrey picked it up because she was a bit of a neat freak. Not that I minded. The woman had quirks—potato chip sandwiches, for one—and every day, I marveled at my luck in landing her.

She stepped forward and unbuckled my belt, her cool gray eyes on mine. Heels brought her up to my chin—almost. "I haven't seen him in a while and he was my friend before he was yours." She palmed my erection, gave it a gentle squeeze that drew my groan.

"Bean. You're killin' me."

She unpacked me, her eyes lighting up at what she found. Like I was a gift she'd requested from Santa. I was big, and fitting her body used to be one of my major concerns.

"I need to change."

"In a minute, Georgia." One-handed, she reached under her sexy dress and pulled down black, satin panties, a feminine skill I particularly enjoyed. Faster than you could say "sex in heels," I was flat on the bed with my beautiful wife straddling me. Did I mention how lucky I was?

"With my pants on?"

"Got to make it quick," she panted, her voice already raspy with desire. "Need—need you so bad," and then she was taking me inside her wet, wet heat and I was trying, desperately, not so desperately, to hold back, to not be my usual beast self because she was carrying my baby.

I pushed up her dress and spanned my hands across her still flat stomach, love and disbelief churning inside me. The changes about to be wrought on this beautiful body were a testament to how much we loved each other.

But sometimes she needed more. She needed promises. "Tell me it'll always be like this."

It was easy to say yes, to say always, to say forever. I believed it wholeheartedly with my foggy head and my full heart and my rampant cock. I'd won the girl of my dreams and nothing could break us.

"Always, Bean. Only you."

She liked me to take charge, so I did. I rolled her over and filled her to the hilt, my care for her situation muffled by my unstinting need. And when we came in quick succession, it felt like something new was created yet again. Each time with her was a revelation.

Thirty minutes later, at every traffic light and stop sign, I couldn't help myself. I had to touch her belly, the swell of life we'd created.

"Grant, she's not going to kick yet. It's much too early."

"I don't want to miss his first punch."

We didn't agree on the gender of the baby and wouldn't find out for six more weeks, at least. She wanted a girl. I didn't mind either way, as long as the little bundle was healthy, but I'd say *he* or *his* to be contrary. Aubrey needed to be challenged at every opportunity, even if it was about something as silly as the predetermined sex of our baby. From the moment we met, arguing was our foreplay.

The sideswipe came out of nowhere, barely a tap but enough to make me hit the brakes and curse the fucker who had driven on blithely without stopping. To this day, I don't think the violent kiss of one piece of metal against another was the reason for what followed. But during long, lonely nights it crosses my mind while I look for someone, anything to blame.

Because it couldn't be my constant need to touch her. Or the fact I'd slipped my body inside her before we left for dinner, the sight of her in that red dress too much for my weak resistance. My uncontrollable lust for my wife couldn't be the reason I'm not a father.

"Prick. I ought to hunt him down, but I'm starved." I gripped the handle. "Better check the damage."

"Grant, I—shit."

My head whipped around to the sound of her voice, its tone unrecognizable and so *un*-Aubrey: fear. Her fingers were on the hem of her dress—that stunning red dress—and the color slashed in a muddy streak over her thighs. Aubrey doubled over, her hand covered in blood. Covered in those cells that hadn't had a chance to become whole yet.

"Fuck." I cupped her face. "Hold on, Bean. I'll get us to the hospital."

The images from that night should be etched on my brain but after the sideswipe, they're patchy. I remember this:

Carrying her into the emergency room as she tried to hold her thighs together.

The doctor, who looked no more than twelve, telling me she was okay, she would be okay.

But.

Aubrey looking so helpless in a hospital gown five sizes too big for her.

My stupidity as I said the one thing I shouldn't: *We'll try again.*

We wouldn't. We couldn't. Aubrey turned in on herself. My job had always been to coax her out of that brittle shell.

Go on a date with me.

Stay in Chicago with me.

Be mine forever.

Faced with Aubrey's pain, I packed away my own in service to managing hers. There was no reason why we couldn't conceive again. No reason why we couldn't give it another shot after an appropriate time of mourning. No reason why we couldn't find our way back to each other, except the biggest reason in the world.

It takes two.

And when I realized I only had so much strength, and that my partner, my love, my Aubrey couldn't meet me even ten percent of the way, I had to bail.

Yeah, I was a coward.

But I can't say that. I can't confess to her that I'm as much to blame.

Of course I don't tell all of this to Max. I don't tell him that it was the night we canceled dinner with him. I don't tell him that I made love to my beautiful wife just before it happened. But I do I tell him enough to understand the broad brushstrokes of a marriage that failed.

"We tried to get back to us, but it didn't work. You'd think in our business we'd know all the tricks—talking, counseling, the healing power of time—but it was like we couldn't apply any of this BS we're always telling clients to ourselves."

"You're in the middle of it, man. The playbook goes out the window."

"I know I should have told you but—"

"Aubrey wouldn't want anyone to pity her." Max knows her pretty well. "I totally get it."

"She's obsessed with perfection, or the illusion of it. Failure isn't an option with that girl."

"Never helped you didn't need to crack open a book. Always pissed her off."

My laugh is mirthless. "That's what she said. But she's been applying that comparison to everything. Like I'm able to grieve more easily than her or somehow figure it all out in a way that makes sense. I'm not and I can't." She didn't even know about my possible part in it—how my rough handling of her might have contributed to the loss. I didn't want to complicate the healing by adding that wrench to the mix.

"But this week has opened things up between us and we're talking now."

"So the next step is what? You two back together?"

He sounds as skeptical as I feel. A few turns in the sack and a little pillow talk does not fix a marriage's problems.

"She's pretty fragile right now and being around her family is doubly raw. I'm conscious that decisions made in this kind of pressure cooker might not stick. For now, I just want to support her while she comes to terms with it."

A sound from the other room alerts me to Aubrey's return. "Gotta go. See you when I get back."

"Sure, and Grant?"

"Yep?"

"I understand that this might seem more personal to Aubrey because she physically carried the baby but it's okay to acknowledge your own hurt as well. Don't try to bury that while you're trying to fix her."

Instead of acknowledging the advice, I latch onto the part that pisses me off. "I'm not trying to fix her."

"Sure thing, white knight. It's been your mission since the day you met her."

I have no response to that, and Aubrey working the handle means I have to ring off with a muffled "thanks." I open the door to find Aubrey frowning.

"Sorry, I thought maybe you'd left," she says, as if I have someplace else I want to be.

"No, Max called to wish us happy Thanksgiving."

She nods, distracted. "I don't understand my mother. She's making all sorts of excuses for my dickwad of a dad. After the stunt he pulled tonight."

"And you thought she'd want what? To talk it out like besties?"

"No. Maybe. I don't know!" She paces the room, hands on hips. "She has to be hurting, and if anyone knows how it stings to be neglected by my father, it's me. I have all this insider knowledge and we could be bitching together."

"And while she's bitching about him, you two might be getting a little closer?" I put my hands on her shoulders and kiss her forehead. "I love that you're trying with her, but damn, she's a piece of work. She got you all twisted up for years and I hate to see you wasting precious goodwill on someone who doesn't deserve it." I'm a firm believer in surrounding yourself with people who love you and cutting out negativity. I understand it's not so easy when it comes to family, but Aubrey needs to start looking after herself better.

"But it might make *me* feel better. Or help me understand some of the decisions she made as a mother. She's always been such an enigma." She smiles up at me. "My whole family's weird. Bet you wish you'd never bothered."

"I dunno. Perks are okay."

"You mean, mashed potatoes and onion gravy, which I'm totally craving. Want to raid the kitchen with me, inhale a vat of rum-spiked eggnog, then fuck each other until we pass out?"

"Yes, yes, and hell, yes." I kiss her softly to let her know I'm in her corner. I will always be on her side, and she sure as hell doesn't need the Gates to make her whole.

CHAPTER 21

Aubrey

I awake rested but alone. Within seconds a bolt of panic streaks through me.

Where is he? And how annoying is it that I care?

Blinking to full consciousness, I focus my eyes and spot the Post-it on the pillow, right in the depression where Grant's head lay last night.

I'd just reached a point where I was doing okay alone, and now I'm twisting and turning with lust and affection. Those two together equal something I don't want to acknowledge: I never stopped loving my ex-husband. And while I don't doubt his affection for me, I suspect it's more kindness than a true intention to win me back. Grant needs to fix me before he can move on with his life. I'm the mission he failed, and leaving it incomplete—*me* incomplete—offends his good nature.

God, that's depressing. I refocus on the Post-it.

Come to Libby's. –G

Fifteen minutes later, I walk into my grandmother's

apartment and head toward the noise coming from the kitchen. Utter chaos greets me, with Grant at the center of it.

"Aunt Aubrey!" my niece Caitlyn screams on seeing me, which sets Asta off running in circles and barking. "We're making French toast!"

More like she's wearing French toast. Her fingers and hair are covered in gooey egg mess. Thatcher isn't much better, though he's stuffing his face with bread, which somehow seems more productive than just wearing raw egg.

"Hey, no eating the brioche," Grant says. "That's for breakfast."

"Uh, I know," my cheeky nephew replies.

"Why, I oughta . . ." Grant catches my eye and winks. "About time you joined us, wife."

Wife. There goes my heart again. Dead, not getting up.

Libby is sitting in an armchair at a safe distance from the action, sipping from a Red Sox cup. I doubt it's coffee. Cat Damon is curled up in her lap. "Slept quite late, Aubrey? I assume you have a good reason." She chuckles evilly. "That husband of yours doing his duty, I'm sure."

"Libby." I raise an eyebrow to acquaint her with the presence of children, not that that would ever stop her.

I have to admit Grant's relationship with my gran tickles me something wicked. They're such an unlikely pair yet that's Grant for you: he's always known how to adapt to any situation and roll with the punches. Unlike me, who can't seem to get out of her own way long enough to find that sweet spot. Maybe it's why we work—or used to.

"So when's breakfast ready?" I sidle over to Grant and stand close enough to touch our arms together. Strange how this feels as intimate as when he's inside me. It's the domesticity of it, I suppose.

He's just doing this because he cares. As a friend.

"Breakfast is ready as soon as Thatcher sets the table."

Thatcher explodes. "Why do I have to do it? That's a girl's job!"

Grant shuts that down real quick. "No such thing. There are only jobs, and none of them are more a girl's than a boy's."

"That's not what my dad says."

I slant a glance at Grant, wondering how he'll handle it. "Well, how about we look at it like this? You set the table and your sister will clear the plates away. That's fair, right?"

Neither my niece or nephew look like this is fair at all.

"I guess you don't want breakfast, then," I offer to the negotiation.

"Fair 'nuff," Grant says. "More for us." He nudges me, clearly pleased at our teamwork, and that smile—oh, God, I'm in deep.

A plaintive cry cuts into the happy buzz. Minnie is in a bassinet on the other side of the table, and somehow I totally missed the little button.

"Wait, where are your parents?"

"Mom and Dad went into the city to shop the Black Friday bargains," Caitlyn says.

"Why aren't they doing it online like everyone else?" I walk over to Minnie and pick her up. She's so small and helpless. "You need to be fed"—I sniff—"and more."

"Perfect timing," my grandmother says with a cackle. I suspect the woman has never changed a diaper in her life. Too busy adventuring and imbibing.

"I've got her," Grant says, taking Minnie from me and holding her at arm's length. She gurgles and giggles, thinking it's a game. "You take care of the coffee, Bean."

My heart is at risk of cracking in two, maybe three or four. Blinking to hold back tears, I reach for the French press in the cabinet. Grant's left the room to change Minnie, and the older kids are doing as they're told, setting the table. I can't believe Janice and Tristan left them behind, but I'm not a parent—what do I know?

"You've got a good one there, girl."

Sure, state the fucking obvious, Gran! "He's all right, I suppose," I mutter irritably.

"So when are you going to tell me what's going on?"

I turn with that squinty-eye thing people do to stop them from losing it. "What do you mean?"

"You and Grant? You're not fooling anyone, honey."

"We're fine."

She holds my stare over her mug. "Okay, have it your way. I'll be here when you need to talk."

Regretting my crankiness, I lean over to kiss her, amazed that the frail ninety-year-old in the wheelchair is a hundred times stronger than me.

"Back in a second," I murmur, needing to escape.

It's stinky in the living room—Libby would have a fit if she could see Grant using her very expensive Turkish rug to change the baby on—but I may as well be sniffing roses because Grant's currently destroying my ovaries in one fell swoop. He's talking to Minnie like she can understand every word.

"What's that, sweet pea? You got somethin' to say?"

Gurgle, gurgle.

"Nah, now you're just bein' silly."

This conclusion is met with a flurry of giggles, and isn't that the most beautiful sound you'll ever hear? This should be a torment, but strangely, it's not. My irritability falls away. My mind's caught up to what my heart has already accepted.

I lost something precious but my life doesn't have to end.

He finishes up, skills he learned from when taking care of his sister, all the while talking to Minnie in low murmurs. When he turns, he looks surprised to see me.

"Didn't see you there." His tone is shy, careful.

"That's okay, you had your hands full." I rush forward to take the soiled diaper.

"Nah, you take care of your niece. I'll get rid of that."

The weight of her in my arms is perfect. I never thought I'd have a maternal bone in my body but as soon as I got pregnant, the joy overtook the fears. As soon as I lost that child, the fears returned and solidified into the status quo, a narrative that fit. I was undeserving. My body understood that I didn't have it in me to nurture, that this life I'd fallen into with a wonderful guy like Grant was an accident.

"She would have been about eighteen months by now," Grant's voice says behind me.

Those words would have sent me into a flood of tears months ago, but not now. "Seventeen months, three weeks."

"Do you think about her?"

He doesn't say the name, but I feel it floating between us. *Riley*. I'd imagined we would have a girl, though it was too early to know. Either way, we both liked the name Riley, which could apply equally to either gender.

"I think about her all the time," I say, my eyes trained on my bubbly niece. "What she might have looked like by now. Whose eyes she'd get. Whether her hair would've been straight or curly. Would she have my temper or your easy-going nature." I think about love and loss and all the ways we hurt each other. "Do you?"

"Sometimes, but mostly I think about you and what a great mom you'll be."

"Grant—"

"Listen, Bean." He moves closer, his strength lifting me with every step. "Sure I think about the baby we lost, but I can't do anything about that. Grief and love are inextricably combined, but while the love remains, the grief becomes more muted, I suppose. Time and tears. I'd rather think about the beautiful woman who will one day feel ready to take a chance again. I want you to start thinking of the future, Aubrey."

I'm paralyzed by his words, which should be liberating. I've been feeling a spark lately—a sexual spark, sure—but that doesn't mean it extends to remaking the rest of it. What Grant says sounds lovely but it also sounds like a back-handed way to push me forward.

Just as I suspected, Grant is healing me for a future without him.

He watches me with those midnight-dark eyes. Will I shut down or will I fight?

There's another option, a middle ground: take what's happening here and just enjoy it.

For the next three hours, we are run ragged between preventing the kids from eating Great-grandma's special brownies (*oh, that's where they ended up*) to halting World War 3 when Thatcher rips the head off one of Caitlyn's four Barbies (*Zombie Barbie's looking pretty good* is Grant's way of smoothing it over).

"I don't know how Janice copes," I say after we put Minnie down for a nap in one of Libby's bedrooms and the older kids are parked in front of *Coco,* which Caitlyn claims she's already seen "eleventy million times."

"I'm gonna guess multiple nannies are involved." Grant smiles. "We got suckered."

He pushes my hair behind my ear and brushes my chin with his thumb. I must have Nutella on my face.

"You were great with them. Told ya you would be."

It hurts to even think about it, the possibilities of success and of failure. I don't think I could go through that again. Because if I fail—and there's a really good chance I will—crazy Aubrey will be back. The woman who can't see the good standing in front of her because she's chasing the perfect. I know myself too well.

The way Grant is looking at me isn't just sexy as hell, it's telling me I'm forgiven. So foolish. This man shouldn't give me a pass on the pain I caused him.

"Oh, look at you two being all adorable!" My sister-in-law Janice barges in, her arms filled with packages. "Did you wear the little monsters out?"

"Uh, they wore us out," I say. "Now I need a long bath and a giant glass of wine."

Janice plonks down on the nearest sofa. "Oh, that'd be heaven. If only you had a gorgeous husband to provide. Oh, right, you do!" She waves at Grant in case there's some doubt about who she's talking about.

I've always liked my sister-in-law.

I hitch an eyebrow at my ex-husband. "Is she right? Can you provide?"

Grant's thinking on it in that slow, lazy way of his. "I've got a better idea."

CHAPTER 22

Grant

"Only a country boy would think coming into the city the day after Thanksgiving is better than a hot bath and sweet, sweet alcohol."

"And only a Yankee would whine about it."

With her non-slinged arm, she gives me a gentle shove, not much heat to it. She might be complaining but I can tell she's pleased to be out of the house.

We took in the light show at Faneuil Hall and now we're wandering around the stalls looking at knickknacks and tchotchkes, hot chocolate cups warming our hands. I'd thought that Aubrey would be on edge around the kids, especially Minnie, but no. She actually appeared to be enjoying herself. Seeing her play at favorite aunt gave me all the fucking feels, that's for sure.

"Oh, ornaments with names on them!" Aubrey picks up a green one with "Zoe" painted across it in silver script. "Just like the ones on Libby's tree. Would your sister like this?"

"She'd love it." I'm tempted to urge Aubrey to come home

with me, deliver it personally, and bask in the warmth of my family. She needs to be wrapped up in all the love she missed as a kid.

"I don't see one with 'Sherry' on it. But it looks like they take custom orders." While the stall owner wraps up the ornament for my sister, Aubrey asks about the process for ordering a special design. "I'll send it to your mom. If you don't think she'd mind."

My momma might be protective of me but even she can recognize a wounded animal for what it is. She always liked Aubrey, knowing instinctually that she needed mothering. "She'd be honored to receive it."

As we walk away with her purchase, I can tell she's nervous and building to say something. I give her time; it's what she's always needed.

"You talked to Max last night and I was sort of distracted and didn't follow up."

"Uh-huh."

She nods, then swallows. "Did you tell him what happened?"

"I did. He's never pushed before but last night . . . I don't know, it felt like the right time to share with a good friend."

"Because we're talking about it more."

Yes, but also because I think I handled it wrong when we were together. Keeping it all inside did neither of us any good.

"Sunlight's the best disinfectant. That's what my momma says, anyway."

"So, you'll tell her next."

I stop and steer her to the side, out of the path of shoppers and tourists. "Eventually. Just like I think you need to talk to your family. Maybe not all of them, but Libby, for sure. People want to be there for you, Bean. You need to give a little and let them in."

"You think that's the answer. Give a little bit."

"Like the song. It's a start." There are so many ways to begin again, but it requires an action.

"Oh my God." Kind of an odd response, but then her eyes widen as they redirect beyond my shoulder.

Aubrey's father and Mercedes are standing near a whoopee pie station, poring over the choices behind glass. They're wrapped up in each other, oblivious to the world around them.

Aubrey pulls my hand to move away. "Let's—oh, hi!"

Mercedes has spotted us and is dragging Jeffrey over. "Hey there! Aren't these crowds nuts? What have you got there? Doing a spot of holiday shopping?"

Mercedes babbles for almost a minute, obviously nervous. It's clear she wants Aubrey's approval. Hey, don't we all?

After a little small talk, most of it out of Mercedes's mouth, she says, "You should come to dinner with us."

"Oh, no, that's fine!" Both Aubrey and her father speak at the same time, then quickly clam up as they realize they've objected in unison to spending any more time than necessary with each other.

I catch Mercedes's eye, note the pleading expression, and make a decision.

"We'd love to join you for dinner."

Every beginning needs an action.

Fifteen minutes later, we're seated in a nice Italian restaurant in the North End, the scents of garlic and herbs making my mouth water. Mercedes and I are doing our level best to keep the conversation going, but I'll tell y'all: it's a struggle. Until a little bowl of olives is placed on the table and Mercedes comes out with this gem:

"I really enjoyed your article on children's rights during divorce, Aubrey."

Although it's highly unlikely the entire restaurant actually stills with the introduction of this information, it certainly feels like a bomb has just exploded.

Aubrey blinks. "Excuse me?"

"Your article in the *Journal of Family Law Practice,*" Mercedes says blithely, picking up an olive and examining it before returning it to the bowl. "I thought your take on the unspoken property rights of children was an interesting one, especially given that most jurisdictions give it such short shrift."

"Um . . ." A speechless Aubrey is such a rarity that I can't help an evil chuckle." She looks at me in confusion. "Wait, did Grant put you up to this?"

"Mercedes is second year law at Harvard," Jeffrey offers.

Speechlessness gives way to openmouthed gawping. "You're in law school? Why didn't I know this? Did you know this?" She turns to me.

"Might have," I mumble, enjoying myself far too much.

Jeffrey smiles and kisses Mercedes on the cheek. "You think I can't catch a smart woman, Aubrey?"

"Well, Dad, your track record—"

"Is maybe best left unexamined. At least at the dinner table." Regret clouds his eyes and he squeezes Mercedes's hand. "I know I've made mistakes. In all areas of my life."

"None of us are saints," Mercedes says, but it's not unkind. She turns back to Aubrey. "So I'm not what you expected for your dad. Or maybe I'm exactly what you expected. Either way, I'm probably going to be around for a while."

"God, I hope so!" Jeffrey blurts out a little desperately.

Mercedes gifts him with an indulgent look that makes it very clear who's in charge. She's young, beautiful, intelligent, and has her whole life ahead of her. On paper, she doesn't need Jeffrey the way he so obviously needs her, but the heart makes those decisions for us.

Aubrey takes one good, long hard look at her father, then turns to the new power player at the table. "Tell me about your favorite class, Mercedes."

~

I WAKE with a large weight on my chest—a large, furry weight.

"M*#%" comes out of his throat. Cat Damon is making scarier-than-usual eye contact and reaches for my chin with a paw. When Aubrey and I still lived together, this was an easily understood message.

Cat hungry.

My phone screen says it's 2:14 a.m. I wait, pondering if I have the energy to beat the cat at his own game.

"M*#%$###!"

"All right, all right, let's get you something to eat, you little fucker."

Aubrey doesn't stir beside me, so I take a moment to watch her. She looks so calm and untroubled while she sleeps, exhausted after I loved every inch of her. I think she enjoyed dinner with her dad and Mercedes more than she cares to admit. Nothing is resolved but a step has been taken.

As it takes about ten minutes (I'm only half-exaggerating) to get to the kitchen in the Gates Gothic Funhouse, by the time we arrive I'm a tad hungry myself. Except I'm not the only one hunting out a snack in the middle of the night.

Marie-Claire is sitting at the kitchen island looking like Lady Macbeth in Chanel. She's sipping eggnog and looking at an iPad.

"Oh, sorry," I say. "Didn't expect anyone to be here." I turn to leave.

"Not up for spending a moment with your mother-in-law? No, wait, former mother-in-law."

I ignore the jibe. "Just don't want to disturb. Looks like you're taking some time for yourself."

Marie-Claire makes a strange sound, halfway between a laugh and a snort.

"What's so funny?"

"Time for myself. It seems I am an expert at creating it, *non*?"

I don't disagree with her. Time in her presence is usually fraught, and no one appears in a hurry to spend much of it with her. A pang of pity for her gnaws at me, so to slough it off, I start pulling open drawers, looking for a tin opener for the cat food I grabbed from his upstairs stash. It's slow going because I'm doing it one-handed with the cat cradled in my other arm. Either I'm protecting him or he's protecting me.

"What do you need?"

"Tin opener."

Marie-Claire opens a drawer I haven't tried yet, extracts the tool, picks up the cat food—and yanks the ring pull. I laugh at my dumbassery; she merely smirks.

She takes care of filling a bowl, and when the cat's settled she speaks again. "Would you like a Croque Monsieur?" At my blank look, she translates. "A grilled cheese and ham sandwich."

"Sure."

In all the years I've known Aubrey, I've spent maybe ten hours total with her mother and about ten minutes of that alone with her. You might say we've got Aubrey in common, so that should be enough, but when one party's goal is to keep a boot on the neck of my woman, then it's hard to find middle ground.

Apparently it's a night for surprises because her next

statement catches me off guard. "How is Aubrey sleeping these days?"

"Better."

With deft moves, she removes ingredients from the fridge: bread, ham, cheese, something in a covered bowl. "She used to have nightmares as a child about getting left behind in places. At home. At the store. At school."

"Doesn't take a psychology degree to figure that one out."

No comment on that. She constructs the ham and cheese sandwich and slathers a layer of thick cream sauce from the bowl onto the bread.

"What's that?"

"Béchamel. It's not a true Croque Monsieur without it. The proper way is to bake it but I am taking a shortcut." She drops the sandwich into a pan of melted butter, the sizzle as mouthwatering as the smell.

"I would sing *'Frère Jacques'* to coax her back to sleep." She slants me a look. "This surprises you, *non*?"

"Nothing surprises me, Marie-Claire. You've never struck me as completely heartless. Everyone's got their reasons."

She flips the sandwich, showing off the lovely golden-brown crust. "Cultivating independence in children is important, but especially in a daughter. Whoever she chose would eventually hurt her. That independent streak would be her saving grace."

Because better we all make peace with the fact we'll be dying alone anyway. What a crock. "So seeing me rear my ugly mug again is the last thing you want."

She places the sandwich on a plate and slices it in half, taking one for herself and pushing the other half my way. I pick it up and bite into it, savoring the gooey Béchamel sauce complimenting perfectly with the salty ham.

"This is delicious," I murmur around bites.

"I don't make it much. I don't make much at all these

days." She takes a seat at the island and considers me. "I can't say I'm all that happy to see you, Grant. Aubrey would be better off with someone less—"

"Southern?"

"Emotional."

This makes me laugh because I consider myself to be the calmest, most even-handed person I know.

"You think this is funny, but it is true. There is something of the sentimentalist about you, Grant. Not to mention a crazy-eyed view of love that can give a girl ideas. The wrong ideas."

"That she deserves to be adored and worshipped. Yeah, pretty radical thinking there."

She smiles over her eggnog. "And when you let her down . . ."

"I won't."

"You already did. If you love my daughter so much, then why did your marriage fall apart?"

This is usually the point in my internal dialogue where I give all the credit to Aubrey for being walled off and inaccessible. Where I backfill the blame game to include the woman before me and the asshole who bought me dinner tonight. Psychologists and therapists would talk about cycles and repeating patterns, but what it boils down to is faith—or lack thereof.

I'm not going to share what happened with Marie-Claire; that's Aubrey's story to tell. But I will tell her this:

"Humans live constantly in the moment, needing instant gratification to keep those happy-sappy neurons firing. And during the bad times, we're looking for this quick rebound, and the happy memories, those good times should be a storehouse you can draw from. Only this time the bank was closed and all the ATMs were vandalized." Marie-Claire is watching me carefully. "I'm not making much sense. Neither of us trusted that the good was enough to tide us over the bad. Aubrey and I have problems but they're our problems, for us to work out, together. Don't need anyone interferin' or offerin' rebound guys or uninvited opinions."

"M#@%&!"

"That goes for you, too, Cat."

Marie-Claire takes a sip of her eggnog. "Well, perhaps you are worthy of her after all."

I can't tell if that's meant as a compliment or an insult.

BROOKLINE COUNTRY CLUB is the oldest club in the United States, so exclusive that the list of people it's rejected for membership is more famous than who it's allowed through its hallowed doors. These fuckers wouldn't even let Tom Brady and Giselle join until they begged (or gave up one of Tom's championship rings, I'm guessing).

Of course it's the site for Libby's ninetieth.

Like so much in Boston Brahmin culture, everything is a bit faded and decrepit. The upholstery is chintzy, the furniture old, shades of money long spent. Country clubs are part of a bygone age, and given Libby's practicality and brook-no-bull attitude, it's hard to tell why she buys into it. She's a cut above this lot.

So is Aubrey, who looks like a dark angel, wearing my favorite color on her, a ruby red with a dip of the fabric to reveal her back, which means no bra. Jesus.

"What are we doing here?" I ask as we walk in. "When I'd much rather find a closet and run my hands inside that dress."

"Just one more night and then you're free to go."

"Come to Georgia with me tomorrow."

She turns, her eyes wide and wary "But—no. What would your mother think? Wouldn't that confuse her?"

"She'd love to see you. Zoe, too. I was going to fly and pick you up on the way back but we could leave early tomorrow morning and drive straight through. Or we could load you up with pot brownies, leave Cat Damon here for a couple of days, and just fly there."

"I worry about Libby—"

"Who would like to see you living your best life."

Yesterday we had fun with her nieces and nephew. Sadness pinched us at first but mostly there was us, healing, getting our happy on. Figuring out that once it might have felt like the world ending but that love will find a way.

I will find a way.

I pull her out onto the dance floor because I need to hold her tight against me. I also need the entire congregation to witness me claiming this woman for my own.

"They're a strange pair," Aubrey says, with a nod to her father and Mercedes, who have just appeared at the doorway.

"So she's not a gold-digging bimbo after all."

"Jury's still out on the gold-digging piece, but yeah, she doesn't need my father. He's pretty smitten with her, don't you think? He'd be really hurt if she dumped him."

I laugh. "So now you're worried about him?"

"Oh, shut up. It was easier when she wasn't nice and interesting. I don't think my mother has any idea how serious it is. She thinks there's still hope that it's just another of his late-life crises."

"You need to stop worrying about everyone else. Let them sort it out."

"I can't help it. Better that than think—" She cuts off.

"Than thinking about your own problems?"

She shrugs, her chin dipped, hiding her expression. But that's okay. I know what she's thinking. I always have.

Appropriate courtly rituals are observed around Libby and soon we sit with her, in time for the audiovisual presentation that Aubrey has been working on, the one honoring her grandmother. It's clear that she's led a fascinating life. Some of it I knew: her stint in Hollywood, her aerial exploits, her forays into the business world. More of it was a surprise to me, as it revealed a softer side. Volunteer work with veterans, an affair with a Hungarian count, holding her newborn son in her arms. It was this last sepia-toned image that Aubrey lingered over, as if to prove that even the most brittle personalities are capable of great feeling.

The presentation ends and the audience claps politely. Now would be the time her son would—*should*—stand and toast his mother, but Aubrey stands in his place, the strongest of the clan, and addresses the crowd.

"My grandmother, Elizabeth Amelia March Gates, our Libby, is a remarkable woman." She smiles down at her grandmother. "Everything interests her, nothing fazes her. She's a true Renaissance spirit with beauty, wit, and gumption to match. All my life, I wanted to be more like her. Elegant, fearless, and just a little bit inappropriate."

Boston society laughs at that, the sound like tinkling crystal.

"I've come to realize that there's only one Libby. No one can come close to emulating her, but we can all enjoy how much she enriches our lives." She raises a glass. "Libby, I love you. Here's to seeing everyone back here for your hundredth!"

Over the clink of glasses and the calls of "To Libby!" the woman scoffs. "If there's any chance I live to be a hundred, I'll throw myself off the Tower!" She grips Aubrey's hands, her eyes shiny with emotion, and my heart warms to see my girl getting the love she deserves.

Janice and Tristan are seated near us, though Tristan is on

his phone. Has been all evening. Janice leans in, conspiratorially. "So, when are we going to hear the patter of tiny feet from you two?"

I squeeze Aubrey's hand. "Plenty of time for all that."

"You're getting on, Aubs," Janice continues. "For every year you wait, your fertility rates plummet! I mean, Tristan only has to look at me and I'm pregnant. I'm going to have to get him to snip it—right, T?" She nudges her husband, who doesn't look at her, still busy on the phone. "After this one, I said, baby, no more. The hoo-ha can't take it."

"The birthday girl can't take it, Janice," Libby says. "Put a sock in it."

"I'm just giving them advice, from one old married lady to another!" Janice smiles, and God, I know she means well, but please shut up.

"Oh, Christ!" Libby says, and we all look up to see my father approaching the table with Mercedes.

"Mom," he says, leaning over to kiss her. "Happy birthday."

Libby gives a snort of disgust.

I stand and offer Mercedes my seat. "Oh, thanks, Grant, you're such a gentleman."

My smile is a little forced, the wear and tear of the charade starting to weigh on me. I can't wait to see my own family, and I'm more determined than ever that Aubrey will be with me when I do.

"Drink, sweets?" Aubrey's father asks his girlfriend.

"Just some ginger ale to settle my stomach." She rubs over her abdomen, the gesture so familiar that something inside me jerks hard in reaction.

Maybe no one else noticed.

"Are you—oh my God, are you pregnant?" Janice screeches, dashing any hope I had.

Mercedes colors and gives a shy look at Aubrey's father.

"We're supposed to be keeping it on the down low. It's so early and you never know what might happen."

"Jeffrey, if you were any dumber I'd have to water you," Libby says. "She's old enough to be your daughter. Your *grand*daughter. What the hell are you going to do with a baby at your age?"

"Stay out of it, Mom. Can't you be happy for us?"

Mercedes turns to Aubrey, clearly uneasy. "I'm sorry we didn't tell you sooner. We were all getting along so well at dinner last night and we weren't quite ready to share it."

Aubrey pats her hand, her expression shockingly calm. "It's something you want to hold close for a while. I get it. It's okay. Congratulations."

But it's not okay. I'm tired of this family and how they force-feed politeness and veiled insults down one another's throats. I'm tired of the passive-aggressive nature of their superficial relationships. Mostly, I'm tired of Aubrey taking it all without fighting back.

"What are we congratulating?"

That French-accented voice cuts through the party like a rapier.

"I'm going to be a father," Jeffrey says, as if he's not already one. His eyebrow raises in challenge to his soon-to-be ex-wife.

Marie-Claire mutters something in French, and while I only know enough to say hello, I can tell that what she said isn't nice. "So that's why you want the house. Why you'd like to ensure I don't have my share. Well, I won't be there to raise it if this one gets dumped on you."

Aubrey blanches.

I've had enough. I reach for her. "Let's dance, Bean."

But her grandmother is squeezing her arm, which makes Aubrey stare at her. And stare. Recognition dawns.

Aubrey turns to me, her big eyes rounded and panicked.

Slipping out of her grandmother's feeble grip, she stands, all while glaring me into the grave.

I follow her out to the lobby and catch her before she makes it to the restroom.

"Aubrey, wait."

She rounds on me, fury in her eyes that she can't muster for her dreadful parents. "You told my grandmother?"

"Yes."

Surprised at my unvarnished confession, she takes a moment to collect herself. "The phone call, Elvis's *"Burning Love"* ring tone, that was from Libby. Who else knows?"

"No one. But I'd tell everybody if I thought it would shatter this fucked-up family dynamic you've got going on here."

"It's no one's business! Grant, this was supposed to be ours to get over. To get through."

"And how did that work out, Aubrey? We kept it inside and it destroyed us."

"That's not why. I had it handled and you wanted to dredge it up over and over again. Unnecessarily. And with my grandmother?"

"I told Libby because she knew something was wrong. With you. With me. With us."

Aubrey's a volcano waiting to unleash the molten core's fury. She thinks she can remain dormant but nature will eventually win out. It has to. People pass us by, and all I can think is: *go nuts, baby—scream it the fuck out!*

She's barely breathing, snatching at shallow bursts of air as if she can't get enough to fill her lungs.

"C'mon, Bean, I know you're mad at me. That's okay."

"Don't tell me it's okay," she grates. "Don't tell me what to think."

"Someone has to, because you're unable to express your anger like a normal person. Your mom told you to act like a lady, to not make a fuss, to never let them see you sweat. Your father wouldn't know a genuine moment of affection if it bit him on his cheatin' ass. So you stuff it all down with top-shelf champagne and painted-on smiles and pretend it's all fine when it's fucked beyond all recognition." What will it take to make her go batshit in Boston? "You've been living those rules for so damn long you don't know how to climb out of that pit of perfection you're buried in. But I see you, Aubrey. I see everything you refuse to."

"Quit with the cheap psychoanalysis—"

"Cheap, Bean? Nothing cheap about it. I've paid dearly these last two years. But why bother when I can love you so good we'll both forget all our problems." I hear the sneer in my voice. I hate it but have already committed to my part. Moving closer, I overwhelm her with my brute strength. "That's what you'd like, isn't it? For us to use our bodies to figure this out."

Her breathing is heavy, labored. She raises a hand to my chest, pushing away but holding me close.

"Yeah, that'd suit you better. Don't get mad at them when you can work out all that mad on my cock."

She gasps. "You—don't you dare . . ."

"What? Talk about how you like to use sex to paper over the cracks, Aubrey? Is that not proper talk for the high society party?"

"This is nobody's business but ours."

This. This. Fucking *this* again. "So you keep saying, but your strategy of keeping it to the two of us hasn't exactly worked. We lost a baby, Aubrey. We lost a child we had already started to love, a part of both you and me, the natural result of how much we goddamn adored each other. And nothing I did was right. Nothing I said was good enough."

She's shaking her head. "I just wanted you to hold me. Desire me. Love me."

"And I did. I loved you so much. But you wanted me to love you with my body instead of my words. Well, that's what got us into trouble in the first place, Aubrey! I couldn't keep my hands off you and our baby is dead."

Her eyes go wide. Shit, I—*shit*. That wasn't supposed to come out like that. It wasn't supposed to come out at all.

"Grant, what are you talking about?"

She touches my jaw and I recoil in self-disgust. The last time we fought like this, I fucked her in a diner restroom, pouring all my anger into sex that won't solve anything in the long term. I can't do that again.

I'd expected that Aubrey would play her part and be the one to walk out of this argument. For the first time in fuck-knows-how-long, that privilege is mine.

CHAPTER 23

Aubrey

Grant walked out on me, and I'm trying to wrap my head around it.

It's okay.

God knows we've hurt each other and it's about time he told me off for being the crazy one in this relationship. But what he said . . . he can't possibly believe that, can he?

I exit the restroom corridor and run smack into my mother. The look on her face makes it very clear she heard every last word of that exchange with Grant.

"Here to make this all about you?" I snap.

She doesn't even look surprised, which means that maybe Grant's right and I should have lost my shit with her years ago.

"What happened, Aubrey, with the baby—I wish you had told me."

"Why? So you could tell me how disappointed you were that I couldn't even get that right?"

Shock crosses my mother's face. Of all the things to move her . . .

"*Cherie,* I don't know what to say," she says, for what might be the first time in her life.

I don't have time to soothe her. All I can think is that Grant needs me. For years, he's been holding on to my shit and his own. Hearing this from Marie-Claire is an irony I'm not quite ready to wrap my head around.

He's not in the foyer. He's not in the bar. I spot him outside talking to the valet.

"Grant!"

His body freezes and he speaks without turning. "Go back inside. It's too cold."

"We have to talk." I move around to face him.

"No. No, we don't. We're all out of words. That's what you want, right?" He takes off his jacket and throws it over my shoulders, which is so fucking Grant.

"I need to know what you meant. About not being able to keep your hands off me."

His face twists in pain just as the valet arrives with his car.

"I can't be here, Aubrey. With these people. With this toxicity." He looks over my shoulder. "You should go back inside."

The implication is that I belong with the toxic people. I don't. I belong with this man who fills up my soul and never leaves me empty.

"I'm coming with you."

Instead of arguing, he opens the passenger door. I step inside, so does he, and then we're off, a twenty-minute drive weighted with a crushing silence neither of us seems capable of breaking. I want to question him about what he said but it seems really important to focus on navigating the icy roads without dying. In my head, I try to parse the words.

I couldn't keep my hands off you and our baby is dead.

Grant's always been so aware of his size. He's a big, husky guy who is completely in charge of his body—and mine, too. He's never hurt me but he seems to think . . . oh, God, he thinks he might bear some responsibility for what happened that night.

Back at the house, he parks and exits the car, stalking toward the house. Whether I follow doesn't seem to concern him, but I do. Of course I do.

Inside, it's quiet as the grave. "Grant, stop."

He turns, and we stare like we're seeing each other for the first time. I want to ask him a million questions, poke and pry and pick at the scabs. But mostly, I want to feel everything he does.

We fly at each other, clawing and hungry, hurt and on fire, smashing our mouths together.

"I'm sorry," he whispers as his tears mingle with mine. Tears for what we lost and what we've missed. All this wasted time when we should have been healing together.

"No, please," I beg, not sure what I'm urging him to do.

Don't apologize.

Don't take this on your broad shoulders.

Don't stop loving me in all the ways I don't deserve.

He slips a strong arm under my thighs, lifting me into his steady embrace, then takes the stairs two at a time. I love his strength, the obvious physicality of it and the less obvious internal fortitude that keeps his heart so steady.

"Grant, I—"

"It's okay. No more talking," he says, though it's the opposite of okay. I've made a mess of everything. He's offering to do it my way, use our bodies to express it all. I've worn him down and made him come around to my way of thinking, a victory I can't in any way savor.

The next few minutes are hushed and urgent, weighted

with the knowledge that we can't go back and forward is just as uncertain. We're caught in this no-man's-land of lust and pain.

His hands move across my nakedness, first with care, then with necessary roughness. It's how I like it. How I've always liked it, and that he should have beat himself up over how he touched me that night . . . oh, my love.

I grasp his ass and mold him to my body. "What you need, baby. Everything you need."

He's inside me before I've spoken the last word, filling me so completely because his cock belongs there. Is part of me. He's squeezing his eyes shut, but I wouldn't dream of closing mine. I don't want to miss him pumping all his strength and emotion into me. I've always loved to watch him, especially that moment when he's close to bringing me off. He gets this slight, smug twist to his mouth.

But not today. Today's different because everything has changed. We're not the same. We're not better but we're better together.

"I love you," I whisper, and those words I've withheld so long cause his eyelids to snap open. All that heated blueness. They're liquid and filled with more than lust.

"I love you," I say again, concerned he hasn't heard me. Really absorbed the words.

He thrusts harder and I arch up into him, the orgasm building and sparking and conquering me so fast I didn't see it coming. But he's not finished with me.

He slips out and turns me over, his brute hands spreading my legs for his pleasure. I'm expecting a hard thrust—I welcome it—but that's not what I get because Grant has never played to my expectations. Now his soft tongue bathes me in love, each flick over my sensitive tissues a beautiful torment. Still no words, only our desperate moans filling the air.

It doesn't take long—it never does—and soon my heart and lungs are flying apart, scattered to all corners of the room, the earth, and the heavens beyond. Before I can seal my organs together again, he's back inside me in one brute stroke. But it's gentle, too.

It's Grant, my protector.

Still buried in each other, we fall to the bed in a spoon. Grant covers my breast with his big hand while he leaves no spot inside me untouched. Every corner found, nowhere left to hide. His hand moves up to my chin to turn me toward him, ensuring I see everything he wants me to see.

He doesn't tell me he loves me. I know it with every stroke inside me, with every grunt from his throat, with every flash of those eyes.

I know it because he's crying.

His body shakes when he comes, then goes as still as the air around us. I try to hold on to consciousness—it seems important to stay awake in this moment—but I slip away into the sleep of the guilty.

When I awake, he's still here, his gaze on me, keeping me safe.

"Sorry, I didn't mean to fall asleep."

His smile is everything. "I worked you good, Bean. It's okay to rest. It's only been an hour."

So everyone is still at the party. Good. Grant and I need to talk before the circus comes back to town.

"What you said before about taking the blame for the baby—surely you don't think that?"

He closes his eyes for a moment, then reopens them slowly. "Sometimes, I was rough with you. You're so tiny and I loved dominating you, my big oafish body ruling your petite frame. And that night, I couldn't help thinking that I'd had some part in it. And I couldn't fess up, so I tried to stay away from you after. Be careful."

While I was spending my mourning period trying to reseduce my husband, he was battered with guilt over the imagined role he'd played in our tragedy.

I curl my hand around the back of his head and pull him close. "Nothing you did caused the miscarriage, Grant. It was just one of those things. Some weakness in me—"

"No. Don't take this on. Not again. It wasn't your fault."

Ah, but . . . "It wasn't the first time."

He leans up on his elbow, his eyes blue flames. "What do you mean?"

"It happened in law school. In our second year. I didn't even know I was pregnant, but I had awful cramps and thought it was just a really bad period. Stressed about exams or something." The words gush out of me with a whoosh that sucks in all the air around us. "But I was late and it was at the wrong time and—"

"Did you see a doctor?" he snaps.

I nod. "She said it was probably a miscarriage, that it's more common than you'd think. I didn't want to worry you. It seemed easier to try to get past it. Move on."

"Easier." The word is quiet. Lethal.

My heart's flapping like a baby bird's wings. "I didn't want to put that on you. Another problem."

He sits up, leaning thick forearms on his knees. "This had happened to you before, years ago, and when it happened again you didn't want to burden me with it? We were going through the shittiest time of our lives, unable to communicate, barely able to crawl through the pain, and you wouldn't even tell me this funda-fucking-mental thing that was tangible, that we could focus on to get over the hump. That maybe we should be doing more medically or talking about it from a different angle."

"I was too caught up in the present. In what was happening to me now. Then."

Disgust dims his eyes, and I realize I've made a huge mistake.

I should have given him that. Told him everything so it would absolve him of any guilt he might be feeling. But I didn't even realize he was carrying that.

Because you didn't ask, Aubrey. Because you don't know how to.

"I knew I had this problem and when I realized it might be the thing that destroyed the dream you had of a family—"

"You were the dream, Aubrey! I wanted you. The woman who loves me enough to tell me her deepest, darkest fears. But you know what? She doesn't exist. She's a figment I invented because I was blinded by the rest. The out-of-my-league beauty who graced her favor on the southern boy. I'd love if she had my children, but if we weren't blessed, we could have figured out a solution because there are a million kids out there in the rotten world who need loving parents. But you know what else they need? Parents who talk to each other. Who don't keep it all in like they win prizes for who can shore up the most secrets and who can internalize the most pain."

He rips back the covers and stalks around the bedroom, picking up his clothes.

Terror quivers through me. "Grant, I screwed up. I know that. But spilling my guts is new to me. It's taken me a long time to get to a place where I can do it."

"So you've said. But we were together for years, Aubrey, and you still never opened up. Not fully. You can blame your family or your upbringing, the pots of money or the goddamn country club, but when I needed you to give a little, *you* decided it was on a need-to-know basis." He stabs his legs into his suit pants.

I don't know what to say to him. It feels like we're stuck in our one true fight, fated to go around in circles. I'm closed off and unavailable. He's the paragon of communication I can't appreciate. Two archetypes that can never meet in the middle.

He's right. I don't deserve him and I'll never make him happy.

He grabs his shirt off the floor but doesn't put it on, torturing me with the sight of his strong chest—the one I may never get the privilege of touching again. "I'm heading to Georgia."

"Okay."

A sad, disbelieving headshake. "That's it? Just okay?"

"You're better off without me, Grant."

"You fucking coward."

The words strike me like an open-faced slap, though I deserve them fully. I deserve worse.

Two seconds later, he's gone.

CHAPTER 24

Aubrey

A plate of brownies whisper to me from their spot on the coffee table in Gran's apartment. I suspect they're riddled with pot.

"Jordie makes these for you?"

"What else is he going to do all day while I nap?"

Fair point.

I'm tempted to get high on my grandmother's illegal baked goods but I figure the glass of wine in my hand is more my speed.

I can't believe he left me. Again.

You drove him away. Again.

"So, you've gotten yourself into quite the pickle, girl."

"Every time I think we're moving forward, I do something to lock us waist deep in mud."

She sighs and takes a bite of her brownie. You'd swear the morsel sends her soaring on contact if her starry-eyed look is any indication.

"You should have told me, darling. About the baby, the divorce, everything."

"I'm not like you, Libby. I might aspire to your level of no-fucks-given but it's just not in me to share like that."

"You mean overshare?" She laughs warmly. "I know I talk too much and embarrass the hell out of you. I never expected you to be the same but I hoped . . ." She trails off, her disappointment in me obvious.

"I'm glad you were there for Grant," I say, truly meaning it though the initial reveal hurt. "In a way I couldn't be."

"Did I ever tell you about the airman I had an affair with in 1943? He was going off to the front and there I was, the prettiest of all the March girls . . . They called us the Wild Ones because we were unstoppable. I would have enlisted myself if they'd let me fight with the men. You girls today have it so easy. Can do whatever the hell you want."

Sometimes I wonder if my grandmother hears a word I say. How is this related to anything that's happening right now?

"Marvin McTavish was his name," she continues. "He had a crop of red hair and the carpet matched the drapes, I can tell you."

Oh, God, I so don't want to hear about my grandmother's sexual conquests, especially when they're made up. Marvin McTavish, my ass. "Is there a point to this story?"

"I'm getting there!" She sniffs, which I don't buy, considering the source. "He died within twenty minutes of getting to France."

"Wait, in 1943, you would have been only 14!"

"I know, I was a late developer. Marvin kissed me and said, "Don't forget me, Lizzie. And I said, "Don't call me Lizzie, you shithead. It's Libby. You never listened to a word I said."

I wait for the punch line, fairly assured this will be a long one.

"Thing is, Grant *did* listen to you. He listened to you too well and he let you make all the decisions about how this situation would play out. You dictated the schedule, the release of information."

I know all this. "You're supposed to be making me feel better."

"You want to feel better? Eat a brownie! You want the truth, then listen to what I say." She leans in and holds my chin. "I tried my best to make sure you weren't like them, Aubrey. But you were too damn stubborn. You thought that shell of yours was a strength when it was really a weakness. Grant figured out how to get you to drop the act. He never wanted perfection because he thought he'd already found it. With you, scars and all."

I swallow my emotion, feeling like I'm choking on it in my effort to hold it all in.

"I lost a baby, Libby."

"I know, darling. And I'm so sorry."

All that pain and emotion I've been keeping in bubbles and burns. Libby puts a bony arm around me and pulls me close.

"But worse, I lost the one person who wanted to be there for me. Because I wouldn't let him." My throat feels thick, my nose itchy, and then they come: those elusive tears. "I've made a complete mess of everything."

"You were always so hard on yourself, darling. Like you had to prove you deserved your place here, when really you were worth a hundred of them. I see that and so does Grant."

"I'm—I'm too walled off for him. He needs someone softer. A nurturing type."

My grandmother looks skeptical. "One nurturer per relationship is enough. Let Grant play to his strengths—taking care of you, putting up with your nonsense—and you give him what he needs."

Which is what? Every marriage needs contributions from each partner. What gaps do I fill for Grant?

In answer to my unspoken plea, Libby says, "Passion, humor, drive. It all skipped a generation and went from me to you. But you shouldn't have to go it alone, not when you have a man like that ready to step up. Just let him love you the way you deserve."

Thing is, I don't believe I deserve it, not from Grant. And until I realize my worth, what I can contribute to this relationship, then I'm not sure I can be the woman Grant needs me to be.

~

PACKING UP, I turn at the sound of a knock on my bedroom door.

"Mom!"

She looks behind me as if she expects to find I have company. It's only Cat Damon, who mewls at the sight of a visitor. "May I come in?"

"Of course." I stand aside to allow her to walk past me. She takes a seat in an armchair while I sit on the bed.

"Well, well, well, all this drama!" She flicks a hand dismissively. "Your father yet again making it about him."

"I'm sorry you were embarrassed at the party. I know that's the worst thing that could have happened."

She looks at me quizzically. "Worse than my husband leaving me for Kathy in Human Resources all those years ago? Worse than finding out my daughter has been carrying this pain and chose not to tell me?"

"Mom, we're not that kind of family. I'll be honest and say you're the last person I would ever confide in."

A brief flash of something—pain, perhaps?—shadows my mother's face but she quickly schools it like the pro she is. "Do you ever wonder why I did not encourage the mother-daughter confidences? Why I have sent you out on your own and expected you to fly without my help?"

"It had crossed my mind." My voice is shaking.

"Because I have always had faith that you would be the woman I could never be. Independent, strong, unconcerned with propriety. You were my miracle child and—"

"I was your what?"

"We all know your father is eminently fertile. Did you ever wonder why we had no biological children of our own?"

Because . . . she couldn't. I'd always assumed she just wasn't all that maternal. My heart catches hard. "Why didn't I know this?"

"It was not necessary. Or . . ." She pauses, tilts her head. "We just didn't talk about these things. These days, everyone is so willing to share on Facebook and the Tweeter—" She waves a Gallic hand. "But back then, we didn't have the same outlets. I was new in the States, friendless, a pariah for stealing the heart of a married man. They all looked down on me, those women at the country club. Your father was useless, didn't want to see a doctor. Didn't see the importance of it when we already had the boys. And then came you."

The words gush out of me. "I was forced on you. Dad's mistake, the defining symbol of his infidelity. How could you even stand me?"

Her eyes shimmer. "Perhaps I have not been as outwardly loving as I should have been. I did not want your father to think he had won, I suppose. The boys were always so needy—they are boys after all—but you, Aubrey? So independent, always striving. Determined to make it on your own. I admired you for it, and perhaps resented you for being the woman I could never be. So unconcerned with what anyone thinks."

"I cared what you thought!" But do I still? I stand, needing to be upright to express this. "I've always cared and I thought I was a constant disappointment to you. You hated that I became a lawyer—"

"A divorce lawyer, Aubrey."

"You hated that I married Grant."

"I thought it dangerous. The man is obsessed with you."

In a way Dad was never obsessed with her. "Is that the problem? Are you jealous?"

"Green with it, *petit*." She smiles as if this excuses everything. Before me is some sort of shape-shifter, a chameleon inventing new arguments for whichever wrong she feels should be defended in the moment. None of it makes a cohesive defense and, dammit, no one knows the laws of emotional baggage like I do.

"You can't do this. You can't wipe away years with a confession about the baby you couldn't have and that I somehow failed to adequately replace. You can't tell me you wanted me to be independent and in the next breath tell me my makeup isn't right or I'm not wearing the right fucking gloves. And you certainly can't tell me that you don't like my husband because he loved me too much. No. Nah-ah. Not going to fly."

She lets out a breath. "Nothing I say is what you want to hear."

"How about an apology?"

"You are right. I—I didn't know what to do with you, this beautiful girl who proved my husband wasn't the problem. He found a woman to give him a child and then he expected me to clean up after his mess."

"Me. The mess."

"Yet . . ." She looks thoughtful, as if the word she just

uttered wasn't in any way hurtful. "I loved you the moment I met you all while hating myself for my failure. And if I was to be your mother, then I would mold you into the child I wanted. But you resisted. Always."

Tears threaten; my throat is tight. "My childhood felt like a battlefield. Torn between trying to please you and seeking Dad's wandering attention. I didn't know about your loss. But I understand that it must have been awful to have to raise the child of your husband's mistress. I wouldn't wish that on anyone, but it wasn't fair of you to punish me for it."

"I took it on but perhaps not as wholeheartedly as you deserved." She squeezes my hand, but it can't make up for how small I feel. How inadequate I've always felt. One conversation filled with excuses and halfhearted apologies can't absolve a lifetime of feeling like crap.

I withdraw my hand.

I haven't always felt unloved, however. Libby made those early years bearable. And then I met a boy, a wonderful southern boy who gave me his heart on sight. Who never doubted me even as I doubted myself.

Grant has always treated me with such reverence and love, it breaks my heart to realize I don't deserve him. But this knowledge has an upside. Having experienced a relationship built on love and respect, I know I can help my mother.

"Mom, you deserve so much better than Jeffrey Gates. Let me help you put an end to this and get back your self-respect."

"Aubrey, that's not nec—" She catches herself, perhaps recognizing that her stale denials will no longer stand up in a court of law. I've seen something in her—something redeemable—and there's no stuffing it back in the bottle. "You shouldn't have to concern yourself with that. I will resolve it."

"I want to. I want to give you the benefit of my legal expertise and life experience. You don't have to go through this alone." I hug her and for the first time in I don't know how long, she squeezes back, an acknowledgment of our new and fragile bond. One I hope will strengthen as we learn how to be honest with each other at last.

CHAPTER 25

Grant

"About time you showed your handsome face!" My mother grabs my jaw and pulls me down to kiss her. "Heck, you've gotten taller than a Chicago skyscraper."

I stopped growing at sixteen but Sherry tells me this every time I see her. "Somethin' in the Windy City water." I say that every time, too.

Jake appears behind my momma and reaches around to offer his hand. "Grant. Good to see you."

"You, too. Happy Thanksgiving. Sorry to get in so early. Or late." It's two in the morning and I was lucky to catch the last flight out of Boston. "I just had to . . ." I shake my head.

"Hon, what's wrong?" Momma is all concern, her blue eyes shimmering. "Is it Aubrey?"

"Yeah, but there's more. Where's Bug?"

"She's staying over with friends. We thought you weren't coming in until later this morning. She'll be furious she's not here to greet you."

"Might be better for the moment. Momma, I need to tell

you something." I drag in a ragged breath. "I need to tell you why Aubrey and I fell apart."

Eighteen minutes later, I'm knocking back my second beer and cringing at my momma's tears. Thankfully Jake's there to do his job and soothe.

"You should have told me," she sobs.

"I know. But I thought I was protecting Aubrey. She's so contained and while years with me has opened her up some, she's still this girl with the Yankee code. Get on with it. Don't dwell. It's not healthy but it's how she was raised."

Jake rubs my mom's back and says to me, "Thanks for telling us, Grant. I know it must be hard for you to talk about."

"It is, but it's been getting easier. Aubrey and I hashed it out, finally. I thought we were getting somewhere, but it's two steps forward, five steps back with her. When it happened, I tried to operate on her level but it just—it just came out of me one day when Libby called. I'd been holding it in." I grasp Sherry's hands. "I'm sorry I confided in another woman instead of you, Momma. I was trying to be strong for my wife and then one phone call and it came tumbling out."

Sherry won't hold it against me. The woman wouldn't know a grudge if it packed a punch. "I'm just glad you shared it with someone, hon. No one should have to bear that alone."

That's how I'd felt, flying solo in this grief bubble made for two. And now I'm angry all over again that my wife would put me through that. If she had told me the truth—not just that it had happened before but that she was going through hell—then maybe we could have figured this out.

"Aubrey's still in Boston," Jake says. "So where do you two stand?"

Back to square one. Though that's not entirely true. We made some strides these last few days, but I don't know what it means for us. I just know I had to get away from her before I said something I couldn't take back.

"She thinks she can't be enough for me. Because she failed once—twice—and I know she doesn't want to go through that again. But I could've told her that was never the goal."

She was the goal. It was always her and everything else was gravy.

And now? I have no idea.

"Do you like it?"

I regard the bracelet comprised of shocking pink and neon orange beads my sister has just made for me and pull on the elasticated band to test its strength. Unfortunately it holds.

"Love it, Bug."

She gives me a sly smile. "Time you tapped into your feminine side."

Little huckster knows exactly what she's doing.

"Suits you," Jake says with a laugh as soon as Zoe heads into the kitchen to help my mom.

"It's my own fault for getting her a jewelry-making kit." I take a draught of my beer and turn back to the Falcons game. We're getting our asses handed to us, which fits my mood just fine.

"Can't believe how big she's getting," Jake muses. "Seems like only yesterday I was changing diapers, terrified if she shed a tear, afraid to go to sleep in case something happened to her and I couldn't be around." He catches my eye, his expression changing from nostalgia to concern.

"It's okay," I say, allaying his worry that he's stepped in it. "I can talk about babies and not fall apart." It's Aubrey I can't reckon with right now. For two years, I've lived with the guilt of how I might have contributed to her miscarriage. Two years of misery without her. When I tried to talk to her, she kept the pertinent details to herself—we have a name for that in the law. It's called nondisclosure of exculpatory evidence. My then wife elected to keep the fact of her prior miscarriage to herself.

I'd like to have known to make myself feel better.

But mostly I'd like to have known so I could make *her* feel better.

"Mind if I ask you somethin' personal?"

Jake's expression says he minds big-time but he merely mutters, "Go ahead."

"My momma's a pretty independent woman, so I'm guessing that might have given you some trouble when you started this."

Jake's frown turns to a smirk. "You could say that. She'd lived her whole life doing it her way. Insisted we split the bills at restaurants. Wouldn't let me fix her damn toilet without calling around first to find out the going rate for a plumber so's she could pay me that and then some. Hell, when she got pregnant, and I asked to marry her, she said no. Twice."

I smile because I've clearly hit a sore spot. "How'd you get through to her?"

"She had to come at it from her own angle. Figure out where we fit together and what we could do for each other. It took a while for her to let her guard down. Open herself up to me." He sips from his beer. "Your Aubrey's a tough nut to crack, I'm guessin'."

"You guess right." But we were getting somewhere in Boston. Everywhere she was surrounded by slings and arrows: cute-as-button nieces and nephews, Janice hassling her about having a baby, her mother's condescension, her father's immaturity. I'm supposed to be her rock yet here I am, miles away.

Did I bail too soon, not give her the chance she deserved? But what about the chance I deserved, the one she refused to offer to let me heal her? Christ, I hate feeling like this. Bitterness is most definitely not my jam.

My phone pings with a call from Lucas. I really should ignore it, but having my brain sandblasted with his inanity seems as good a distraction as any.

"Think this is about work," I tell Jake as I head into the parlor for privacy. "Yup?"

"Well, cheerio to you, too, mate!"

I growl. "Not in the mood, *mate*."

"Listen, I had a call from one of your clients . . ." He launches into a lengthy monologue about how a client needed a shoulder to cry on in my absence and how he now thinks I ought to be giving him some sort of holiday bonus. I reckon this ridiculous convo has some purpose, but I don't have the energy to cut him off. He'll get there in the end.

Significant cough. *Finally.* "Max told me about the baby, Grant. I'm really sorry for your loss."

"Thanks. It was a long time ago, though."

"Yeah, I know, but I imagine it's still pretty raw this week now you're hangin' with your ex. I wish you'd spilled. I could've helped, if only to make you laugh. I'm told I'm quite amusing."

"You mean, like you opened up about Lizzie?" His twin sister died a few months ago after being bedridden in a nursing home for over a decade. I've known the guy for seven years and found out about her existence a month ago.

"Touché," he says easily, which makes me feel guilty for snapping at him. "But now I talk about her all the time. Trin can't shut me up." He takes a breath. "I can recommend a therapist."

"The only person I've ever wanted to talk about this with is the one person who can't. Who insists on following her own blueprint for grief. I can't make her open up about it. I've tried." Things were starting to turn in my favor this last week, a small step toward my dreamed-of future. "How did you get over it, Lucas? Losing this person who was such a big part of you?"

"I didn't," he says without hesitation. "I don't want to. I want to keep her here." After a pause, he adds, "I'm touching my chest in a most heartfelt manner, by the way."

I laugh, wondering at how little I truly know him. You spend all this time with someone but their interior workings remain hidden, too complex to navigate properly.

"See, I am exactly what you need, mate!"

"Oh, fuck off."

"That's the spirit! Listen, Grant," he says, his tone lower, graver. "This thing about Aubrey insisting she follow her own blueprint for grief—that's okay. There isn't one way to mourn. Everyone handles it differently and it isn't always linear. Sure, shrinks will tell you that there are stages and maybe you've reached acceptance and Aubs is still stuck in depression. Or every now and then you go back to anger because this person was taken away from you and it's just so bloody unfair. Not just because you've lost them, but because it forced you to change how you feel. That's a lot for someone as controlling as Aubrey to handle."

He's right—and whoever thought I'd say that about Lucas? Aubrey's emotions have always operated on an even plane, a defense mechanism she's employed to control her life. I've usually had an easier time tapping into my inner resources. Comes from having a mom who was constantly asking me how I felt about stuff. We're that close, that I'd be more likely to tell her than not.

But Aubrey? Losing our unborn child forced her to

acknowledge feelings she'd been trying to suppress forever about her neglectful father, her cold mother, and all the pain she's kept inside about her upbringing.

Lucas is still talking because that's what the man does.

"Now that all the feelings are out in the open—they are out in the open, right?"

"Yeah, they're running around naked and taking big bites out of the scenery."

"Mega! So it's this big mess of shit that's spewed all over everything. Stinking up the place. It had to get really ugly, it had to break out of its confines, it had to—"

"Lucas, could you get to the point? If you have one?"

He tuts. "You are testy, mate. What I'm trying to say is that you needed to blow it up before you could heal the rift. But it won't be the same, Grant. It can't be."

I think on this. "I just want it to be 'us' again. Grant and Aubrey. What we had." In this I think Aubrey and I are in agreement. We want to return to the certainty of "before."

"Maybe this is your new normal. Instead of thinking that you have to land on the big X that marks your previous state of happiness or what you thought was your perfect life before this big event, maybe you just acknowledge that life is too messy for such clear-cut compartmentalization." He chuckles. "Bloody 'ell, say that ten times fast!"

I want to accept this wisdom even though it doesn't fix my current problem: Aubrey and I are miles apart, physically and emotionally.

And I fucking hate that.

"Hey, thanks. For calling, for listening, for—you know. Being an annoying friend."

"Anytime. Multiple pints on you at the Frog and Footman when you get back. And yes, I'll handle your client calls because you can't be arsed to. I'm much better at it anyway."

CHAPTER 26

Grant

"Kind of early for this," I mutter to Jake, low enough so my little sis doesn't hear. "Isn't it?"

"You'll be gone tomorrow," Zoe says, having heard me loud and clear. "So we have to do it now."

We're trimming the tree the Monday night after Thanksgiving, and frankly I'm more than holiday'ed the fuck out. I'm flying back to Boston tomorrow to pick up my car, which means I need to figure out if that will include Aubrey and Cat Damon on the return trip. I want to see her—I always want to see her—but then, I'm a masochist to the bone.

"Here, have some eggnog." With a wink and a smile, my mom shoves a small cup in my hand, which is undoubtedly laced with rum because that's how she rolls.

"I'll be back for Christmas, Zoe."

"With Aubrey?"

I squint at my sister. "No. Aubrey and I aren't together anymore."

"Maybe you can bring her a present. I made her an anklet!"

The doorbell chimes and Sherry makes a move. "That'll be Gary and John from next door. I told them to stop in for a drink." Inviting all and sundry to drop by is my momma's favorite pastime.

I hear a screech, then multiple feminine laughs. Not Gary and John, then. The follow-up soundtrack is the movement of people and then the most surprising sound of all: a sorrowful, scratchy mewl I'd recognize anywhere.

The damn cat.

I head out into the hallway and lock eyes with a pair of silver-gray beauties.

"Aubrey!"

"Yes, I'm here!" There's a hitch in her voice that I attribute to nervousness. She puts down the cat carrier while my mother rolls her luggage to a cubby under the stairs.

The next few minutes are spent taking Aubrey's coat (the red one I love), commenting on her cast (the sling has gone), seating her on the sofa *(Oh, you're trimming the tree! It's gorgeous!),* plying her with eggnog (with lashings of rum), and generally ensuring our guest's comfort.

"Do you mind if I let him free?" Aubrey gestures to Cat Damon, who's scratching at his carrier. "He won't go for the tree. He doesn't like the smell."

Because it's kind of awkward when your ex-wife shows up at your childhood home unexpectedly, everyone seems glad of the distraction to deal with the feline. Zoe takes care of making sure the cat feels at home, though I monitor him closely because the surly little bastard could get even surlier.

"Aubrey, how did you get here?" I'm guessing she drove straight through, leaving not long after I did.

"I flew!"

"What?"

She giggles, and the sound pinches my heart painfully. "I took a plane. Well, I didn't actually fly the plane myself. That'd be crazy and it's not as if I could learn to fly a plane in less than forty-eight hours. I'm also a bit . . ." She lowers her voice—or she thinks she does. "Tipsy. But I'm sobering up nicely."

"You are absolutely fine, hon!" That's my mom. "We need to get her something to eat. Jake, put together a plate of turkey and mashed potatoes. No green beans, because Aubrey doesn't like them."

Aubrey's eyes go wide in a way that tells me she's trying to hold back tears. "You remember that?"

"Of course I do! It was like a federal case one year you visited and then because you wouldn't eat them, Zoe thought she didn't have to."

"Still hate them," Zoe says in solidarity, though a green bean hasn't passed her lips since she was two.

Aubrey cups Zoe's face. "You've grown up so much. So pretty. And Sherry, I don't need anything to eat right now. It's just so wonderful to see you all." Avoiding my stare, she takes another sip of eggnog. "Hmm, rum. I hope you don't mind me barging in."

"You are always welcome here, Aubrey." Mom again.

"You shouldn't be so nice to me, Sherry. Not after everything I did to Grant."

"What did you do?" my sister asks, her voice alive with concern.

"She didn't do anything," I say in her defense because I will always protect her.

"I wasn't very nice to him. Made his life hell, actually." This time, she finally looks at me.

"Oh, you guys had a fight," Zoe says matter-of-factly. "Mom fights with Dad, but he always apologizes."

"Not always," my momma says, sounding slightly embarrassed. "I apologize sometimes, too."

In response, Jake coughs significantly, which makes everyone laugh except Zoe, who doesn't get the joke.

"I can't believe I flew," Aubrey says. "I couldn't get a commercial flight but one of Dad's friends has a plane and after a small fortune exchanged hands, they agreed to fly me up. Or is it down?" She shakes her head. "Anyway, I drank two vodkas at the airport bar and then two more on the plane. I really needed to talk to you, Georgia."

"I was heading back tomorrow to pick up the car," I say. "I didn't like how I left things. It was wrong."

"No—no, Grant, it wasn't. You had every right to do that. Every freakin' right to call me out on my sh—uh, shenanigans."

"Let's leave these two to talk," my mom cuts in before ushering Jake and Zoe out the door so quickly my head spins. Just as I'm about to say something—not sure what just yet—Sherry barges back in and wraps Aubrey up in a hug.

"We're so glad you're here, Aubrey. We love you so much."

At which point my ex-wife, the love of my life, my beautiful Bean, loses it.

Oh. Shit.

She cries on my mom's shoulder with big, body-wracking sobs, and I'm left standing there like a lump on a log, obviously in the way.

The door to the kitchen opens about fourteen inches and a box of Kleenex appears as if suspended midair. I grab it, muttering my thanks to Jake, and wait there like a human tissue dispenser. Finally they separate and Sherry grabs some tissues, a couple for herself and more for Aubrey.

"Okay, now I'll leave you two for a nice chat."

Nice chat? How the fuck do I follow that?

Aubrey takes a seat on the sofa and blows her nose. "God, your mom is just the best."

"She is." I sit beside her, tissue box in my lap, waiting . . . just waiting.

She hauls in a breath, evidently building up to say something. It might be the vodka talking—okay, definitely the vodka talking—but I'll take any route to honesty I can.

Aubrey faces me with her lovely, tear-puffed eyes. "I'm sorry. For not telling you about the first time it happened. For not opening up when it happened again. For letting you think for even a second that this might have been your fault. For being so self-centered as to assume it was all mine. I don't know if we can fix what's broken, and I'm not here to ask for us to go back to what we had. I just need you to know that I'm figuring stuff out. Or trying to."

"That's good. Great." Because it is.

She smiles. "You know that movie *Eternal Sunshine of the Spotless Mind*?"

I blink, not sure where this is going. "Vaguely."

"Jim Carrey, who has real acting chops in this one—I mean he really should do more dramas, don't you think? Well, he's so hurt by his relationship with Kate Winslet that he wants to have his memories wiped. He thinks it would be better for him, to help him move on. And this service is available that does that for you. In the future. Or a future that's like our future but different. Memory removal of entire relationships to deal with grief and pain."

I hear what she's saying but I don't like the implication. "That's what you want?"

"I thought I did. I thought that the best way forward would be to pretend it didn't happen. That we didn't happen. Take a scalpel to the whole thing. Excise the *us* out of me."

If I had a chance to do it over, knowing what I know now,

would I? "It'd be better if we could just selectively remove the memories that cut us deep and keep the good stuff."

She smiles again, a little sad. "Unfortunately with relationships, it's all or nothing. We can't ignore the bad just to focus on the good. It lacks symmetry."

"Symmetry. Ruining everything."

Silence rules for a moment while we both absorb this one key truth. She puts a palm over my balled-up fist, which I hadn't even realized was clenched. "I think you thought that this trip, us thrown together, you being the rock you've always been—you thought this would be enough to fix me. That your penis could solve my problems, that your kisses could salve the wounds. Or at least, you thought that doing it my way would open me up to your way. The physical intimacy would lead to the emotional."

"It wasn't my worst idea," I venture.

Her laugh is a melody. "Sex is never the worst idea, especially when it's as good as it is with us. But you were right to accuse me of using it as a crutch. We needed to speak honestly, say what's in our hearts, instead of letting our bodies do all the talking."

She inhales deeply. "I didn't make you happy for a long time. For a while there, I made you incredibly unhappy. I was so wrapped up in my own grief that I couldn't see yours or even acknowledge that you were going through something profoundly difficult. I wish I could change that, remove those memories along with some of the other more painful ones."

"But we can't," I say.

"No, we can't." She raises her silver gaze to me, eyelashes dotted with tears. God, I hate to see her cry, but damn that's what she needs. We need to blow it up and start over, but if it's just more of the same—I don't think I could stomach that kind of failure again.

I thought that knowing Aubrey's failings combined with

my patience was enough for us to overcome anything. But it wasn't. It isn't.

I need to be a little less patient and Aubrey needs to be a little more honest.

"What do you want from me, Aubrey?" My voice sounds rusty, my hurt a palpable thing.

"In that movie, Grant, they meet again on a train and start a relationship, not realizing that they were together before. They're so drawn to each other that not even the memory wipe can keep them apart. And when they find out . . . when they remember . . . they have to decide if it's worth giving it another shot even with all the pain that went before."

"And you think we're worth another shot?"

"I do," she says. Defiantly, almost.

"Well, counselor." I gesture to an unspotlighted point of the floor behind my momma's coffee table, just to the right of the half-trimmed Christmas tree.

"Make your case."

CHAPTER 27

Aubrey

Make your case.

That's what I'm here for, isn't it? I know he's glad to see me, but I also know this was never going to be a slam dunk. I've hurt him too much to assume we can just kiss our way to our happily-ever-after.

Marriage takes work, so time to haul ass.

I stand up, ready to present my argument to the judge, jury, and executioner, all of whom are distilled into the mind and body of this man I love so damn much.

"I'm all sorts of fucked-up, Grant."

He raises an eyebrow, obviously surprised at my opening statement. It's a touch inflammatory and no judge should allow it.

I hurry on. "I'm a scaredy-cat who seeks perfection and expects failure. And for too long, I've thought my Yankee stoicism would get me over every hump. In my family, relying on others was no better than communism.

"You, on the other hand, were brought up to recognize hard work and fair play. That family is important and surrounding yourself with the people you love is the best self-care."

"Objection," he says, half-smiling. "Counselor is grandstanding. Besides, no one's perfect."

I take that small seed, cover it with soil, and let it buoy my hope that water and sunlight, the best disinfectant, can grow it into a tree. Perhaps conscious that important matters are being decided, Cat Damon makes his move and jumps into Grant's lap, where he has a prime view of my presentation.

"We've always had different approaches to our relationship and our marriage, but it worked for us. Sure, I was aware that I'd completely lucked out with this kind, generous, amazing guy who was prepared to put up with my special brand of crazy, but I also knew that I made him happy. He thought I was funny and smart and beautiful. He didn't play games. What I saw was what I got and what I got was what I wanted. We figured out the ideal give and take until . . . until we lost the baby." My eyes fill with tears and Grant—lovely, caring Grant—plants his hands and feet, ready to leap from the sofa and take me in those arms made to love me.

I stay him with my hand. "No, please, let me do this. Let me say this."

He settles again, though every bone in his body clearly strains at the notion of not being allowed to comfort me. Could I love him any more?

"Losing her—and I always thought she was a her—was the worst thing to ever happen to me. Or at least I thought that until I lost you. Knowing you were out there but not in my life properly was like a knife to my gut. I thought we could overcome anything, but we failed at the first hurdle. Most of that's on me. Okay, all of it."

"Bean . . ."

"It's okay, Grant. I'm supposed to be coming up with reasons why I think we're worth another shot but all I can think of is the reasons why I'm so good at hurting you."

"Then get to the good stuff, Gates. Take it home."

I hold up my hand and start a count. "One, we have different strengths that mesh well. I'm kind of a nutjob and you're as solid as they come. I add color to your life. Maybe too much color or drama or—"

"Objection, speculation." And in the next breath, he plays judge. "Sustained."

I giggle through the tears. "Two, Cat Damon is so much calmer when we're together."

We both take a look at Cat Damon, who's watching us quietly like it's just another day in our marriage.

Cat. Cured.

"Three. The sex is fantastic."

"So stipulated," Grant murmurs, low and sexy. Oh, boy.

"Four. I can't guarantee I can change, but I so, so want to. I want to change how I look at things, my coping strategies, my fallback positions. I'm going to start seeing a therapist when I get back to Chicago. A real one, not just one for cats. I want to be a better person, a better partner, just . . . better." The words spill from me in a half-tipsy gush.

His eyes soften, filled with all the love he has for me. "I'll come with you if that helps."

"Maybe it will." Does that mean he wants to do couples counseling? Does that mean we're a couple again? Have I won my case?

I need to make a closing statement. Something that will wow the court.

There's only one thing left to say.

"I love you, Grant Roosevelt Lincoln."

It's the truth, unvarnished and elemental, the simplest of

arguments. For what seems like an eternity, we stare at each other, waiting for the judge to pronounce.

"Can you hold on here for a second?" he asks. "I need to get something. Exhibit A, if you will."

"Uh, okay," but he's already gone. I check in with Cat. "How'd I do?"

"Arghh!"

Two excruciating minutes later, he's back with a small, poorly-wrapped box.

"For me?"

"No, actually." He hesitates, and I see the moment on his face when he goes all in. "For Riley."

I gasp, but it's not pain, only surprise. "Really?"

He hands over the box. One end is lumpier than the other and parts of the inside cardboard show through. Too much tape ensures it will be tough to open.

A two-person job.

In unspoken union, we take a seat on the sofa together. My hands are shaking as I place them over the box, but Grant is there as he always is. My rock, our strength.

"Just rip it, Bean."

I do, feeling as though I'm yanking a bandage off an open wound, but also tearing open a heavy drape to let in sunlight. What's left is a white lidded cube, which I open.

It's a red Christmas ornament, the name Riley blazing across it in silver. My favorite color combined with the hue of my eyes when my emotions take over.

"Oh! From the market at Faneuil Hall."

"Thought you could hang it on your tree when you get home. Start a new tradition."

Or maybe continue an old tradition. I just about manage through the tears, "Could we hang it here for now? Do you think your family would be okay with that? A temporary visit?"

Just like our Riley—with us for a short time before she was taken away to what I hope is a better place.

"I think they'd love that," he says, with such emotion in his voice I know he means *he'd* love that.

Encouraged, I find a spot near the middle of the tree, a stronger branch that can carry the weight of the ornament and all the hope I—no, *we*—placed in our baby. It's a little heavy for it, but with the right foundation, our own tree in Chicago, it could work. Next year, perhaps.

"It's beautiful, Grant." I touch the bauble, nudging it so it catches the light from one of the bulbs.

Grant stands beside me, and I lean in slightly so my shoulder touches his arm. The electricity is still there, ever present, a warm, thrilling hum that connects us.

Facing me directly, he takes my hands. "I've always thought of myself as your key, Aubrey. You were so uptight when I met you, so closed off, and I thought I was the one to unlock you. Unwrap you like a gift. Like I deserved that reward for putting in all this effort with you."

I mentally grimace at the notion I take effort, but he's right. I'm not easy.

He goes on. "But no one deserves another person as their right. People aren't prizes for being princes. I can't save you, Bean, but I still think we can save us."

A sob escapes me. A heartfelt, ugly sound.

"Grant, I don't want to do this alone."

"Then, don't." He cups my hips and lifts me against him and all his solidity and strength. The ballast I need. I fall into his kiss, filled with fire and forever, just as I fell into him all those years ago.

Falling doesn't have to be a bad thing, not when I have the greatest catcher of them all. Life can be joyous, cruel, messy, and terrifying. Love even more so. Rarely is it perfect, and realizing this at long last is the greatest gift I could ever receive.

EPILOGUE

Grant

The not too distant future . . .

Max nudges me with his elbow. "Look at our boy, all grown up."

We both regard Lucas with indulgence, our junior in so many ways. He's standing on the veranda at Max's house on Chicago's North Shore, telling some long-ass tale about Trinity having a cold that could be cured only with Cadbury Creme Eggs. Or something. Other people's love stories are so boring.

"If the fact Trinity thought stopping birth control and *still* letting Lucas have sex with her denotes maturity, then I'll give you that one."

That's right, friends, Lucas Wright is now a daddy. In his arms lies a gorgeous girl named Lizzie with a crop of dark hair and gorgeous brown eyes like her mom's. Our friend and partner in crime is the last one of us to fall to fatherhood.

"So, as Lucas's brain is currently baby mush," Max observes, "it's up to me to do the honors with the quarterly beg. You know there's more than enough work to take on a fourth partner, so whenever you're ready, Lincoln. Time to hang up your Minion slippers and dust off your tie collection. We need you back in the office."

My gaze seeks out my wife, who's standing with Trinity while they both shake their heads at Lucas. She turns and grins, her happiness a tangible thing that hugs my heart.

"I like being a stay-at-home dad."

"Can't think why. Every day I can't wait to get away from the little monsters."

"Daddy! I heard that!" Jessica, Max's five-year-old cuts in. "Billy's the monster, not me." Shaking her blond curls, she pouts and hugs his leg.

Max scoops her up. "Yeah, you're a monster just like your baby brother. I've no problem telling you that. Daddy lies for a living and tells the truth at home."

"Parent of the year award right there,' Charlie mutters on a drive-by to pick up empty beer bottles.

"I want to play with Milly and Ben now," Jess announces imperiously. "Put me down, Daddy!"

"Sure thing, fearless monster, I mean, leader."

She heads off to impose her iron rule over the sandbox Max has built in his backyard, which is about the size of six football fields. I watch her progress until she joins my four-year-old twins. Soon instructions are dispensed for a game that makes no sense to adults, but my little ones take it in stride.

Milly is the strong and silent type, kind of like me. Ben is fidgety and highly strung, more like his mother. They look after each other, which is all I can hope for as they make their way in this crazy world.

Aubrey catches my eye, and we have another perfect

moment filled with love. I'm careful not to use that word "perfect" around her, though. It comes with too much baggage, but in my heart it's what I feel and know we have. My gaze dips to her swollen belly, six months in the making, conceived in the light of a Christmas tree holding a blessed message of hope from the daughter we lost.

My wife, my children, my love, my everything.

I abandon Max and join Aubrey. "You tired, Bean?"

"Not at all. I think Lucas's energy is rubbing off on me."

The mention of the word "rubbing" gives me ideas, not that it takes much to send me there. I splay my hand over her stomach, loving how her breath catches at my touch, loving how my heart thumps excitedly about our future. Our past and present, too, because it's a continuum. No beginnings or ends, only middles. Through good days and bad, each is a tapestry that weaves into the fabric of the life I've always wanted.

"Max trying to get you to come back to work?"

"Yup. You'd think one Lincoln would be enough for him. If we were both there, he'd lose his mind."

"I think *you'd* lose yours if you had to work with me every day."

Aubrey took over my partnership in the firm, a move that made sense for us both from a personal and professional standpoint. We could do the nanny/daycare solution like everyone else we know but this works for us. I missed out on a dad when I was younger, and in a way, so did Aubrey. Having one of us at home fills a gap for us and it's surprisingly fun hanging with four-year-olds.

Not that much different from Max and Lucas, in fact.

"I love my time with them," I say. "Just like I'm going to love my time with this one." Besides, Cat Damon is in his twilight years and does better with company during the day.

At least, that's what I tell myself when he cusses me out for looking at him crooked.

After the miracle of our twins, we had a hard time getting pregnant again, but now we're here, blessed once more. Every day Aubrey comes home from work and I hold her close, ensuring she need never doubt how much I adore her.

I pull my hand away, worried for a moment at the emotional pressure I'm putting on her. She takes it back and covers it with her smaller one.

"Stay," she whispers, one word that encompasses everything.

"You'll tell me if I'm too much."

Her lips curve. "Your too much is all I've ever wanted."

I drag my eyes away from my wife and check in on the twins. Milly is ignoring the latest order from Jessica, instead forging her own path with a wonkily-built sandcastle. Ben is running around in circles chasing Cujo, Max's dog. The future's so bright that if my life was to be freeze-framed in this instant, I'd fall to my knees and thank anyone who'd listen for my good fortune.

"Thanks for holding on," Aubrey whispers. "For never giving up."

My smile takes in all my blessings, the woman of my dreams and the family of my heart. Lawyers usually have no shortage of words, but in this perfect moment I don't need them.

I don't need a damn thing.

AUTHOR'S NOTE

If you or someone you know has suffered an early pregnancy loss, please know that there are resources to help. One such resource is Share, http://nationalshare.org/

ACKNOWLEDGMENTS

Thanks to everyone who gave feedback and advice to ensure accuracy and authenticity throughout the series, including: Andie J. Christopher, Robin Covington, Regina Kyle, Pamala Knight Duffy, and Kelly Jamieson. All mistakes, of course, are mine.

Finally, to Jimmie Meader and Nicole Resciniti, thanks for always being in my corner!

ABOUT THE AUTHOR

Originally from Ireland, *USA Today* bestselling author Kate Meader cut her romance reader teeth on Maeve Binchy and Jilly Cooper novels, with some Harlequins thrown in for variety. Give her tales about brooding mill owners, oversexed equestrians, and men who can rock an apron, a fire hose, or a hockey stick, and she's there. Now based in Chicago, she writes sexy contemporary featuring strong heroes and amazing women and men who can match their guys quip for quip.

ALSO BY KATE MEADER

Laws of Attraction

DOWN WITH LOVE

ILLEGALLY YOURS

Rookie Rebels

GOOD GUY

INSTACRUSH

MAN DOWN

FOREPLAYER

DEAR ROOMIE

REBEL YULE

JOCK WANTED

SUPERSTAR

Chicago Rebels

IN SKATES TROUBLE

IRRESISTIBLE YOU

SO OVER YOU

UNDONE BY YOU

HOOKED ON YOU

WRAPPED UP IN YOU

Hot in Chicago Rookies

UP IN SMOKE

DOWN IN FLAMES

HOT TO THE TOUCH

Hot in Chicago

REKINDLE THE FLAME

FLIRTING WITH FIRE

MELTING POINT

PLAYING WITH FIRE

SPARKING THE FIRE

FOREVER IN FIRE

COMING IN HOT

Tall, Dark, and Texan

EVEN THE SCORE

TAKING THE SCORE

ONE WEEK TO SCORE

Hot in the Kitchen

FEEL THE HEAT

ALL FIRED UP

HOT AND BOTHERED

For updates, giveaways, bonus scenes, and new release information, sign up for Kate's newsletter at katemeader.com

CPSIA information can be obtained
at www.ICGtesting.com
Printed in the USA
BVHW040238150223
658490BV00007B/273

9 781954 107236